JUST CALL ME
SUPERHERO

Alina Bronsky

JUST CALL ME SUPERHERO

*Translated from the German
by Tim Mohr*

Europa
editions

Europa Editions
214 West 29th Street
New York, N.Y. 10001
www.europaeditions.com
info@europaeditions.com

Copyright © 2013 Verlag Kiepenheuer & Witsch, Köln
First Publication 2014 by Europa Editions

Translated from the German by Tim Mohr
Original Title: *Nenn mich einfach Superheld*
Translation copyright © 2014 by Europa Editions

Library of Congress Cataloging in Publication Data is available
ISBN 978-1-60945-229-2

Bronsky, Alina
Just Call Me Superhero

Book design and cover illustration by Emanuele Ragnisco
www.mekkanografici.com

Prepress by Grafica Punto Print – Rome

Printed in the USA

JUST CALL ME
SUPERHERO

I immediately knew I'd been tricked. I pulled my hat back down over my forehead and crumpled up the scrap of paper with the address on it that Claudia had shoved in my pocket—*Family Services Center: Meditation Room*—tossed it to the floor, and I was about to head home again when I saw the girl. She looked at me for a second and recoiled. I couldn't blame her. My own mother had to practice for weeks before she could look at my face without wincing, and this girl didn't even know me. If anything I gave her credit for not throwing up.

Instead of turning around, I lingered in the doorway, pushed my hat back up, and stood there staring at her like an idiot. It slowly dawned on me that I wasn't going to leave. Not now, and hopefully never again. I was going to sit down in the last empty chair, which seemed to be waiting expectantly for me, and I was going to look at this girl. I'd never seen such magical beauty before, those green eyes, that raven black hair—and so sad. She was wearing a very long dress, white with small red flowers, that hid her legs. A short dress would have been fine by me. Brightly colored reflectors shaped like butterflies and flowers sparkled in the spokes of her wheelchair.

I picked up the crumpled paper with the address on it and stuffed it into my pants pocket. I straightened my sunglasses and while the others glared at me, I walked over to the last empty chair.

There were six of us. Aside from me and the girl, there was a long-haired guy with a prosthetic leg, an amorphous doughy figure with a froth of red hair on his or her head (with no apparent disability), a long-legged drag queen with a nervous gaze that bounced around the room, and a frowning arrogant-looking pretty-boy who was wearing sunglasses like mine. Though mine were certainly pricier. He was the only one who didn't turn his face in my direction.

We were each supposed to take a bongo drum and play a rhythm that represented our personality, said the guru as he pulled a box overflowing with pumpkin-shaped objects into the middle of the circle of chairs. Let's do it!

When nobody moved, I thought maybe this place was a good fit for me after all.

The guru was not to be discouraged. He spun slowly around so he could look each of us in the eyes. As expected, he didn't linger on my face for long; it was exactly the opposite when he looked at the girl. I could certainly understand why. What the hell else were we supposed to do here other than look at her? Play the bongos?

How can she stand it, I thought. So beautiful, and the only girl among all these guys. Had she ended up here because she was in a wheelchair and nobody cared what she really wanted? Had her parents put her up to it? Had she been lied to, like me?

The girl shrugged her left shoulder without meeting my gaze. I did her the favor of averting my eyes and looking instead at the others. They all began to shift uneasily in their chairs.

I sighed and directed my gaze to the Lord of the Drums.

It was embarrassing enough that the guru, like me, was wearing a hat. My first impulse was to remove mine. On the other hand, I hadn't been to the barber in ages and the girl was probably having a hard enough time dealing with the sight of me as it was.

Beneath his hat the guru pulled a face depicting a sort of

infinite beneficence. There was something about it that brought to mind an old lady who must have been very cute when she was younger—big saucer eyes that over the years had faded, wrinkles around the eyes and mouth. Set against our grim faces, his cheerfulness seemed somewhat out of place.

"Then I'll do it for you," he said with unbearable placidity. "I'll start with you, Janne."

That's how I learned her name.

I had already suspected that she was stuck up when I saw her small, green eyes. My suspicions were confirmed when she interrupted the guru.

"Stop that," she said. "What could you possibly know about me?"

"Well, then, do it yourself, cupcake," said the guru, rapping a pleasant rhythm on the drum with his knuckles. He smiled so broadly that she blushed.

"I'll start," I said, to get her off the hook. But I was too late.

The kiss-ass in cheap sunglasses had beaten me to it. He had reached up in the air and snapped his fingers.

Marlon was his name, he deigned to tell us. He dragged out the first syllable forever. I looked over at him worriedly. I didn't want to have to share my first name with anyone else. Fortunately, as he moved past the first syllable, it turned out we shared just the first three letters. His voice was calm, almost sluggish, as if he wanted to telegraph with his tone just how cool he was and just how much our company bored him. He'd been blind since the age of seven. That's all we learned. A degenerative disease of the retina, I thought immediately, bad genes, you can never be too choosy about that sort of thing. His family had two dogs, one was this big and the other that big—he held his hands well above the floor. I cringed. For a moment the worn tiles of the meditation room seemed to fall away beneath my feet.

"Seeing-eye dogs?" asked the guru with that typical I'm-actively-listening-to-you face.

Marlon made a gesture with his chin, but it didn't bear any resemblance to a normal nod.

He was very sensitive to smells, he said, pausing dramatically. His nose was unbelievably acute—he could smell what each of us had eaten for breakfast the day before, he said. He asked us to take that into account and pay extra attention to hygiene. And for that reason he was going to change seats now, he said.

The doughy entity next to him exhaled loudly and turned red. I would have felt bad for the person if I hadn't been so disgusted by him, or her.

Everyone watched silently as Marlon stood, picked up his chair, and went to put it down next to Janne. The fact that the fidgety queen was already sitting there didn't seem to bother him. He apparently couldn't see him. The queer grabbed onto his chair and, still sitting, shifted his way into the middle of the circle. Marlon sat down in the vacated spot and turned his face toward Janne, breathing deeply. His nostrils flared.

Janne lifted her hand. I thought she was going to smack Marlon. Which I would have liked to see. But instead she reached over and waved her long slender fingers in front of his sunglasses.

"You really can't see anything?"

He grabbed her hand in midair. "Stop causing a draft," he said, placing her hand on his cheek.

I decided not to come back here again. Despite the fact that I saw Janne smile for the first time.

At some point the guru hit a gong. We stared at him, wondering what he was trying to signal to us.

"That's it for today," he said. The tense corners of his mouth betrayed a genuine sense of relief.

Everyone except Janne and the blind guy stood up slowly,

as if they were unsure they were really free to leave. Then they all hurried toward the exit. I let the guy with the prosthetic leg go in front of me. I was afraid I'd knock him over. Despite the fact that the prosthetic seemed to be shorter than his real leg, he was extremely quick. Maybe he was one of those guys who trained for the Paralympics. His name was Richard, though there was utterly no reason for me to have remembered it.

I bumped into the doughy creature in the doorway. He felt like a jellyfish. It would definitely have interested me to know what sort of disability he had. It hadn't come up. Actually, other than each of us giving our first names, nothing had really come up because the nervous queen had spent the rest of the hour crying and trembling. In the end he'd gone and sat in the corner sobbing.

"I'm a psycho, don't pay any attention to me," he'd said.

The rest of us watched silently as the guru pranced around him with a packet of tissues, a glass of water, and a dropper bottle of Bach's Rescue Remedy. It was the first time I saw something like uncertainty on the guru's face. Now you know what it's like, I thought to myself with mean-spirited glee— maybe you should have trained to become a yoga instructor instead, or learned to lead shamanic journeys or something.

The doughboy had fully intact face, arms, and legs, and he could see, hear, and talk. His name was Friedrich.

I stood aside to let him go ahead of me so he could finally head home and I wouldn't have to look at him anymore. But he did the same thing and smiled up at me. How valiant.

"What kind of a name is Marek?" he asked.

"Polish."

"Are you Polish?"

"No. The only thing East European about me is my father's new wife."

"And who did that?" he asked, gesturing first at my face and then at my hand.

"A Rottweiler," I said.

"But you can see?"

"No," I said, peering past him.

Then I turned quickly away so he didn't somehow think I wanted to chat with him. I went out the damn door and started to run down the hall.

A woman was coming in the opposite direction—not yet old, dollish, and somehow familiar. When she saw me running down the hall she dropped her purse and tried to step out of my way. I had the same impulse and as I tried to avoid her we ended up running into each other. My hat flew off. I picked it up and heard her shriek in horror.

"Please excuse me, I'm so clumsy today," she said and smiled past me. Her chin was trembling.

I wanted to say something nasty to her. But then I realized why she looked familiar: she had Janne's face, or rather, the face Janne would have in twenty or thirty years. I said nothing and ran off.

On the S-bahn train I sat in a window seat and pulled the hat even farther down my face. The car filled up quickly. But as always, nobody sat next to me or opposite me in the four-seat banquette.

I kept thinking I saw Friedrich's tuft of red hair behind everyone who got on the train. Then he would disappear again and I didn't look around to see where he was. If we ever ran into each other again somewhere, I had no plans to say hello. As if I ever went wandering through markets or parks or museums or clubs or gyms anymore.

For once I didn't want to go straight home. I was going to go see Claudia at her office. I wanted to ruin her day as payback.

First I had to get past Marietta, whom Claudia always called her right hand. Even though she, like me, was left-handed.

Marietta stood up when I walked in and braced herself against the edge of the table as if she needed extra strength.

"Marek." She looked up at me and her bright red lower lip quivered a little. I wondered for a second what it would feel like to sink into her lips. I hadn't kissed anyone since the Rottweiler attack. For that alone, every Rottweiler on earth deserved to be skinned alive.

I sighed and took a quick glance at Marietta's cleavage. I liked her because she started talking to me like an adult before I was even a teenager. And because she treated me as if I were her boss, too. Not to mention the hint of red nipple I could see through her not-quite-opaque white blouse.

"It's nice of you to drop by. Your mother is in a meeting right now. Would you like a coffee?"

"I'm in a hurry," I said. She stepped determinedly into my path. I shoved her gently but equally determinedly to the side. I didn't want to hurt her.

"Claudia!" I yelled.

The office was hideous, and I always wondered whether Claudia had purposefully decorated it that way to make clear that she was about work, not window dressing. The hall was long and narrow like an obstructed bowel, the floor covered with ugly gray carpeting; and frosted glass doors rose to the left and right. Between the doors, in square frames, hung paintings that were nothing more than gloomy splotches.

Behind one of the doors Claudia's voice thundered. I had to smile. A Godzilla-like shadow fell across the frosted glass, and then the door sprang open. Claudia swept out wearing a custom-tailored suit. The skirt was way too short for a fifty-year-old. Her makeup was sloppy, her mouth was scrunched up, and sparks flew from her eyes.

"Do we have a problem?"

"I don't. But you? You lied to me." I didn't care whether her client could hear me or not. "It's not a private tutorial on getting my high school equivalency. It's a goddamn support group for cripples with some pathetic wannabe showman in charge."

"Sounds perfect for you." She put the palm of her hand on my chest and shoved me away from the partially open door. Behind the door it was awkwardly silent. Even so, Claudia refused to lower her voice. "I am with a client, so it's not a good time to get hysterical. Take your meds and settle down."

"I only took that medicine for a week—and only because they said it would help with the pain. And that was a year ago!" I raised my voice a bit more. Didn't want the client to have to strain to overhear us.

"Oh, right. Well, then, let Marietta make you a coffee and then go home."

"Why did you lie to me?"

"Why did you lie to me, why did you lie to me! Why do you always say that?"

"Tell me why."

"Would you have gone otherwise?"

By this point I'd allowed myself to be shuffled into the screened-off waiting area, where there was a coffee table with little sparkling bottles of mineral water and orderly stacks of magazines about outdoor living. I slumped down into one of the chairs next to a box of toy blocks. The chair gave a feeble groan.

"I'm not going to go back, just so you know."

"Fine. Just rot away at home."

She yanked painfully on my one undamaged ear and then disappeared again behind the frosted glass. The door clanged noisily shut and vibrated, causing the adjacent doors to vibrate as well. Claudia's apology echoed in the hallway.

With an understanding smile, Marietta offered me a cup of coffee. I sloshed about half of it onto my pants. I still couldn't smile properly—my lips hurt and the skin strained across my entire cheek as if it had been stitched together too tightly.

*

In the car she held the hand with the cigarette out the window and flicked the ash in the wind. The wind blew it back onto her arm and it clung there looking like dandruff. I was waiting for her to pepper me with questions about the cripple support group. And for her to pretend to be interested in the disabilities of the others and then to say that I should count myself lucky because I could walk, see, and hear, that the world offered so much more opportunity for me. She hadn't gone through that routine in a long time.

"Claudia," I said. She looked over at me, surprised at my tone. "If you were a girl, would you run away from me screaming?"

"I *am* a girl." She turned the radio off and put a CD into the slot in the dashboard.

"That's why I asked."

"You know the old fairy tale." It must have been one of her yoga CDs. The car filled with a strange kind of groaning sound. Claudia turned down the volume until it was just a quiet hum.

"What fairy tale?"

"Beauty and the Beast."

I bit down on my lower lip until it tasted salty and still I couldn't feel a thing. There was a time when Claudia kept saying that I didn't look bad at all, that I was almost as good looking as before, that I didn't need to hide myself. That my problem was only in my head. That I had just *convinced* myself that I was deformed. "Look at yourself in the mirror—you're not ugly at all," she'd said time and time again, trying to hold my head still when I turned away from my reflection. "Life is not over because of a few scars, Marek." She said it so often that I began to think I might actually believe her if she repeated it another ten times. Or fifteen. Or a hundred.

And now she was saying Beauty and the Beast. I looked

silently out the window. Outside it was nighttime. I had waited in that screened-off corner, bent over a hunting magazine, until it got dark. Marietta had long since gone home and Claudia nearly locked me in the office. She had gasped and grabbed her chest when I called to her from my spot behind the room divider.

"At least take off the damn sunglasses." She tossed the cigarette away and then pushed the button to close the power window. "You don't want to ruin your eyes on top of everything else."

The following Thursday I was surprised to see that they were all there again. Except Marlon and the guru, neither of whom I missed. Janne was accompanied by the same woman, the one who looked like an older version of her. With legs. She pushed Janne's wheelchair down the long hallway and the old tiles of the Family Services Center squeaked beneath the wheels.

"Hi, Janne," I said as I caught up to them.

"Hi, Mark." She looked up at me briefly and then stared straight ahead. Her mother squinted nervously.

"I can push the wheelchair," I said.

"That's very nice of you." Janne's mother tightened her grip on the handles as if she was afraid I wanted to make off with her daughter.

"Piss off," said Janne without turning her head.

I shrugged my shoulders and let them go ahead.

The self-described psycho queen had brought an embroidered pillow that she was sitting on now. I remembered her name: Kevin. Her lipstick reminded me of Claudia's though she had on more and had applied it much more deftly. Friedrich smiled when he saw me, which made me reflexively reach up and touch my own face. But it was still the same. Richard with the prosthetic had both legs, the real one and the artificial one, up on the chair next to him and was staring blankly out the window.

I entered the room behind Janne. She was met by a flurry

of greetings. For me, nothing. So I didn't bother to say hello either.

"Bye, Mama," said Janne glumly to the woman, who looked around nervously, scanning from one face to the next and fidgeting with her handbag. Janne rolled her wheelchair to the edge of the circle the others had formed with their chairs. There was a space left free for her and an empty chair next to the space. I headed for the empty chair but was stopped in my tracks by a look from Janne. *Not you*, said the look, and I pivoted and headed in another direction as if I'd run into a glass wall. But nobody seemed to find it funny.

Without looking at me Richard lifted his limbs off the chair next to him, freeing up another spot. He looked totally annoyed having to do it, as if I'd begged to sit next to him.

The guru was late. We sat there silently. Janne stared at the wall and looked as if she had turned to stone. Richard read the newspaper. Kevin and Friedrich looked anxiously around the circle trying to make eye contact.

The door flew open. Everyone except Richard looked up.

But it was only Marlon, who I had already put out of my mind.

Now it was easier for me to believe he was blind. He stood in the doorway and rocked on the balls of his feet. He was frowning and his nostrils quivered. I wondered what his eyes looked like behind his sunglasses. Whether maybe he had something to hide. Or maybe someone just told him he'd look cool with sunglasses on, like Agent K from *Men in Black*. Like, a girlfriend or something. He looked like somebody who had sex on a regular basis.

"This chair is free," said Janne quietly. He turned his head in her direction. He went toward with tentative steps, tripped on her wheelchair, and nearly lost his balance. She reached out her hand to brace him but then he managed to straighten up again. I'd bet anything he did it on purpose. Then he grabbed the free chair and let himself fall into it. He stretched out his hand toward Janne as he did but wasn't able to reach her. This time she did not put out her hand.

I wondered whether Marlon realized that everyone was looking at him. Blind people apparently sense that sort of thing. Janne definitely knew that she got stared at, stared at like we were some poor working-class family and she was our TV. But it didn't seem to bother her. Maybe she even liked it.

"Is everyone here?" Marlon asked Janne. She shrugged her shoulders and looked around the circle.

"The guru's not here," said Richard. "He probably needs a new Chinese teacher's handbook."

"Why Chinese?" asked Friedrich.

"Because what I actually registered for was Intensive Chinese." Richard looked wistfully out the window.

"I don't believe this is that sort of course," said Friedrich, sounding unsure.

"Do you think I really do?" Richard rolled up the newspaper and swung it at the wall. Kevin jumped. Something small and black fell to the floor. If I hadn't have heard the crack of the shell I would have taken it for a housefly.

"And you, Janne?" asked Friedrich. "Why are you here?"

She ignored the question. She didn't even look at him.

We heard someone running down the hall. Then the guru was standing in the doorway gasping for air.

"Couldn't find a parking space?" asked Kevin quizzically.

The guru held his chest, wheezing, and leaned against the doorframe. He didn't look just tired but also surprised.

"You're all here."

"Where are the drums?" Kevin asked weakly.

Friedrich was the only one who had signed up to, as he put it, make contact with other handicapped people. The guru seesawed back and forth on the back legs of his chair and listened. As he spoke Friedrich let his little blue eyes rest on me of all people. I crossed my legs, took off my hat and put it on my knee, and smoothed out my hair. Not only had my hair not been cut for an eternity, it hadn't been combed in nearly as long. My fingers kept getting snarled in the matted strands. As Friedrich began to explain that his organs were decomposing because of an autoimmune disease and that as a result he didn't have long to live, I felt sick.

Friedrich happily listed all the medications he took on a daily basis. They had complicated poetic names that he seemed to take visible delight in pronouncing.

"Stop," said Janne when he started to say the fourth one. "Nobody cares."

Friedrich gulped. He forgot to close his mouth and gummed the warm air for a while.

"But we're here to talk."

"Not with you," said Marlon.

Kevin started to tremble again.

The guru cleared his throat and turned suddenly to me.

"Tell me, Mark."

"Marek."

"Tell me, Marek. There was a story in the newspaper a year ago about a fighting dog that attacked a young man."

"Really?" I said. For the first time Janne looked at me for longer than a quarter of a second. For another quarter second I'd probably have to have allowed my entire ear to get bitten off.

"Yes?" I said in her direction.

"Well, I was just wondering . . . " said the guru. Everyone seemed to be listening, his voice hung in the breathless silence, and my back began to tingle. I didn't want them all to stare at me. Everyone always did anyway, but somehow here it didn't seem right. Blind Marlon had even turned his left ear to me and seemed to be straining to listen." . . . if perhaps you would like to tell us about it," said the guru.

I hadn't been expecting such brazenness.

"I remember it, too," said Richard. "It was big news in the paper and they ran a photo of him."

"What kind of photo—before or after?" asked Marlon.

I needed to do something to distract myself from my urge to rip the chair out from under him. So I stood up and left the room and I didn't even care whether Janne looked at me for more than a second as I walked out.

I crossed the street, past all the lit-up shops and bars, and my eyes burned. It happened all the time and it was annoying. I wiped my eyes with a finger without removing my sunglasses but the burning didn't stop. What I really needed was to take off the glasses and dry my face with a tissue, but there were people all around. A class of babbling and giggling elementary school kids passed me. Most of them only came up to my belly button.

They didn't look at me because I was outside their field of vision and thus outside their world, but I could still sense it. Whenever I went anywhere people altered their course to avoid me. The more crowded a place was the easier it was to recognize. Where once there had been chaos, suddenly organized lanes appeared, all seemingly regulated by the same cosmic diagram that had as its goal to get people past me unharmed and with as much clearance as possible. I felt like a clove of garlic in the middle of a stream of ants. People probably didn't even realize they were doing it—their subconscious altered their course in a way that soothed their mind without their ever recognizing what had caused the agitation or what hazard they had sidestepped.

I changed course as well. I went into the first ice cream shop I saw. I'd never particularly cared for ice cream but the bathroom was right at the front of the shop. I slipped in and locked the door. I turned off the light and took off my sunglasses. I felt around for the sink. I thought about Marlon and his question: *Before or after?*

I braced myself on the sink and tears fell on my hands. Crying was ridiculous but when my eyes itched and burned like this there was no stopping the tears. I felt for the faucet, turned it on, and splashed cold water on my face. Somebody knocked on the door.

"Just a second," I shouted and let myself slump onto the toilet seat cover.

One eye itched worse than the other. They probably screwed up and stitched one of the tear ducts closed. Claudia cried a lot at first, always when she thought I wouldn't pick up on it. But of course I picked up on everything. She walked around with a splotchy, puffy face, her eyes squinting, irregular spots of cover cream smeared on, and thought nobody would notice.

And then suddenly she was happy again. Just like that, though I didn't notice exactly when it happened. Like a switch had been thrown. She got used to everything much faster than I expected. She could look me in the face without batting an eye. At first she touched the scars with her fingertips a lot and asked whether it hurt and assured me that I wasn't ugly. She didn't do that anymore.

The bathroom door shook as a fist banged on it.

I stood up, put my sunglasses on, and threw open the door. I saw a young waiter wearing a vest, bow tie, and pants all in black. His mouth opened in a silent scream but something about the shape of his mouth was off. Lip and tongue impairment, I thought to myself. Must have had to go to a speech therapist as a kid. Probably still slurs his speech.

"Boo!" I said and went past him and back out of the shop.

The next morning I discovered that somebody had taken my *Pschyrembel Clinical Dictionary*.

It was my only copy; I'd bought it a half-year earlier at a shop that specialized in medical books. It sat on my bookshelf alongside an atlas of human anatomy, an early-twentieth century book on gynecology and obstetrics passed down to me by my grandfather, and another historical but utterly useless tome with the romantic title *The Art of Healing*, that I'd spared from the recycling bin only because of its beautiful jacket. Claudia had given it to me for my birthday two months before in the hope that my interest in medical reference books might lead to something good and improve our chances of successfully living together.

"See," she'd said approvingly as I unwrapped the book. "It's totally normal for people to discover new horizons after a serious injury. Happy birthday, my beautiful boy."

"Amen," I'd said folding the wrapping paper up nicely. A quick leaf through the tome confirmed my suspicion that Claudia was completely off the mark with this gift. I wasn't interested in the history of medicine. And I didn't want to help anyone. "Thanks for the beautiful book," I said. "Please feel free to borrow it anytime you'd like, for instance if you need a paperweight." She didn't bat an eye.

The history of the art of healing was still there, as was the book on gynecology and obstetrics; *Plastic Surgery: Vol. 1 Basics Procedures Techniques*, an out-of-pocket expense of 229 euros; everything right where it belonged.

But *Pschyrembel* was gone.

I ran down to the kitchen and pulled the plug of the vacuum cleaner, the business end of which our cleaning lady was holding. Frau Hermann was severely nearsighted and also very sickly. She must have been healthier at some point, but I couldn't remember it. The day before yesterday a cobweb fell from the kitchen lamp into my minestrone.

Frau Hermann turned to me. She was very shaky, and her few grayish-white tufts of hair were pulled up on top of her head with the kind of hair clip you expected to see on a Chihuahua.

"Would you like a coffee?" I asked. Her gaze wandered indifferently over my face. She had problems of her own and as a result I felt relaxed in her presence.

"Yes, maybe so," she said.

"On the way." I drew a rectangle in the air. "Have you seen my thick green book?"

"The one with all that nastiness in it?"

"No, the other one. Though it wasn't on the most palatable of topics either."

"Green?"

I nodded.

"It's on your mother's nightstand," she said and turned her back to me. As she turned she made a gesture with two raised fingers. I understood and plugged the vacuum back in.

I hadn't been in Claudia's bedroom since Dirk wormed his way in. Lately I hadn't been talking to anyone; during the day I lowered the shades and napped or flipped through my *Pschyrembel,* and at night I took walks, sometimes even without my sunglasses, and felt the velvety cool air on my skin.

It didn't seem to bother Claudia. She was always in a rush in the morning and Dirk was there in the evening. In between she worked like an animal. Dirk was at least ten years younger than her and he looked slightly stupid though Claudia claimed he was intellectually gifted. I wondered what an adult was supposed to do with his intellectual gifts. Whether perhaps other qualities might slowly become more important, qualities like a spacious apartment with wood floors and a fireplace, for instance. Claudia said I didn't need to worry about Dirk.

That was our last conversation about the topic for the time being.

"My son is in a bad mood," Claudia had said to Dirk just a little too loudly the evening the three of us spent together. In response Dirk asked what I was doing about my depression. I slammed my door shut. I figured he me might as well think I was not only depressed but also violent.

The *Pschyrembel* dictionary was sitting on Claudia's nightstand next to another thick book with a woman with big hair and a beautiful neck on the cover. Beneath the *Pschyrembel* was another book, a thin one that I picked up. It was about post-traumatic stress disorder in adolescents. I put it back down. Then I checked to make sure my bookmarks were still in the right spots in the *Pschyrembel.* It wasn't Claudia's style to rummage around in my things without asking. I was willing to be open-minded: maybe she just wanted to check whether one of her moles looked like melanoma.

I put the *Pschyrembel* back on my shelf and Googled the guru. I would like to have forgotten his name, but unfortunately it was burned into my brain, so I Googled him. I wanted to see whether he happened to be a child murderer on the run for years. But I didn't find any evidence of it. He'd played Puss in Boots at an independent theater and written a book about self-enlightenment through hiking. In the short biography in his book it said he'd been a kindergarten teacher and had survived a life-threatening illness. His Facebook profile wasn't visible to the public. His teaching career didn't show up much, and I couldn't even find our self-help group on the schedule of the family services center.

I typed JANNE into the search box. Clicked on videos. And stayed glued to my screen until evening.

When the doorbell rang the following Friday afternoon, I didn't move from my bed. I watched the fish in the aquarium and imagined I was one of them, like maybe the fat ugly catfish whose entire life consisted of sucking on a round stone. It was so busy sucking that it wouldn't have noticed the end of the world. I envied the fish that.

Claudia was at the office. I hadn't figured out whether Dirk had a job. At least for once he wasn't slinking around our house. I never opened the door for the mailmen. Claudia's mail mostly went to the office and nobody had written to me in a long time. It didn't take much to ensure that nobody wrote me. All I had to do was refuse to accept the huge stack of get-well cards and letters of condolence that the mailman pulled out of his bag a year ago.

The doorbell kept ringing and ringing.

I put my feet into my slippers and went downstairs to disconnect the bell. Through the frosted glass of the front door I could see several shadows.

Jehovah's Witnesses, I thought, lined up for a gangbang.

Now they started banging on the door as well.

"I'm going to call the police," I shouted. "Can't you tell nobody's home?"

Someone pressed his nose to the glass. It looked like a pig's snout, grotesquely distorted and magnified. The banging of the fists echoed hollowly through the entire place.

Okay, I thought. You wanted it.

I averted my eyes from the mirror in the front hall and put my hand on the door handle. I unlocked the door with my other hand. I threw open the door and stepped into the sunlight.

As expected, one of them jumped back and stumbled over his own feet. The other didn't move. I got the feeling that he was examining me from behind his sunglasses. It took a moment for me to recognize him.

It was Marlon, and he was smiling. Behind him Friedrich was getting himself together. He had his hand in front of his eyes. My sunglasses were inside. I wasn't used to so much daylight.

I took pity on my eyes and turned my back to Friedrich.

"Can we come in?" asked Marlon.

"Did I invite you?" I still had my back to them. "How did you get my address?"

"The attendance list," Friedrich peeped.

One of my pairs of sunglasses was on the bureau in the front hall. I put them on and turned toward the two of them.

"What do you want?"

"You didn't come to the meeting yesterday," said Marlon.

"Of course not."

"You were missed."

I thought I must have misheard him. There was no way Marlon had actually said that. So I waited for him to say something more. But he was silent, and it was clear that he didn't plan to give in first. I was the first to get impatient.

"By who? You? Or was it Friedrich?"

Marlon made his chin gesture, the strange nod that said more than a thousand words. I need to remember that, I thought.

"The group. Cut the drama and let us in."

I could hardly believe that they were really here. Nobody had been here in ages. The last 389 days didn't feel like one year and one month or even like ten years. Those 389 days were an amount of time somewhere between a blink of an eye and an eternity.

I hadn't missed anyone, and especially not these two. And yet here they were sitting at our kitchen table and Friedrich's saucer eyes were practically popping out of his head. I could almost hear the rattling in his head. He was taking everything in, the gas oven, the pattern of the dish towel, Claudia's deformed plants in the hydroponic pots, the shelf of spices and valuable antique tea caddies that looked like they'd been salvaged from the garbage. I would like to have had a curtain in front of all of it. Or better yet just to have thrown the two of them out.

Just like Claudia, they began with lies; and just like her they couldn't keep it up for long. I cannot fathom why so many people thought that was an effective strategy. They said something about a special project the guru had planned for us. And supposedly it wouldn't work without me.

I just pretended to listen. In reality I was trying to imagine what Friedrich looked like on the inside. A partially disintegrated thyroid gland. Worn out adrenal glands that had suspended service. Liver chronically swollen from a lifetime of medications. Juvenile arthritis. Shriveled kidneys. High blood sugar. I was tempted to go get my *Pschyrembel* and look up a few more things.

They took my silence the wrong way—suddenly they changed their strategy.

"And Janne asked about you," said Marlon nonchalantly. He was sitting next to Friedrich and running his huge bare feet across the kitchen tiles. Back and forth, nonstop, again and again. I only let them in after they took off their shoes. That was always a good way to embarrass guests. They turned down slippers. I looked at Marlon's feet and wondered whether he cut and filed his own toenails and if not, who had done it for him. Marlon ran his hand along the tabletop and his sleeve barely made a sound as it scraped the surface. It was driving me crazy.

"Janne," I said. They nodded. Friedrich was probably wondering just then whether the grimace on my face was meant to be a smile. I wondered whether they knew how she spent her time. Had she also hit on the idea of Googling their names?

And then Marlon pulled something out of his pants pocket and put it on the table. It was green, flat, and rectangular. I squinted and then reached out my hand.

It was a one hundred euro note.

"What's that for?"

"Forget all that shit we said," Marlon said. "You're going to come because you're getting paid. Consider it work. It's important."

I took the note between my fingers and held it up to my ear. I liked the crinkling sound it made.

"It's not much," I said. "What do I have to do for it? And who is paying?"

There was a pause during which I crinkled the note a little more.

"Well?"

"The guru," they said at the same time.

What they finally explained sounded completely absurd.

"The guru has something extraordinary planned," said Friedrich. "He thinks we all have a huge problem and he wants to help us."

"As far as I'm concerned it would be enough if he helped you."

Friedrich didn't respond.

"What exactly has he got planned?" I asked.

"He hasn't explained it yet."

"Why am I not surprised?"

"First we all have to warm up to each other before it can really start."

"Another disgusting comment like that and you're out of here."

"We're going soon anyway, but you have to come next Thursday. Please. You can't be missing from the picture."

And that's when it finally began to dawn on me.

A dam seemed to have opened in Friedrich. "The guru wants to film us," came pouring out of him. He rushed the words out one after another, choking on them as if he was scared Marlon or I might try to tell him off. But we didn't say a word. I wasn't entirely sure Marlon was even listening. "He might make a proper film about us. A documentary about a group of disabled people. Insights that could break down prejudice, understand? Just imagine, the movie might get reviewed in all the papers and shown at festivals. We could become famous. I even suggested a title. The Magnificent Seven. Great, huh?"

"There are only six of us," I said quietly. "Or do you count for two?"

He smiled placidly. "I counted the guru. In any event, he promised that a big surprise awaited everyone at the end. If he managed to survive it in one piece."

"How nice," I said.

Marlon felt for the note that I had thrown back onto the table and stuck it back in his pocket.

"You just don't get the fact that for once this isn't about you," he said and stood up. "Come on, porky." He turned, touching the wall with his fingertips, and started moving toward the door.

I caught up to them in the entry hall and put a hand on

Marlon's shoulder to hold him back. We weren't finished yet. I didn't fight it when he disdainfully shrugged off my hand and in so doing jabbed his elbow into my side as if by accident. It could have hurt, but it wasn't so easy to hurt me these days.

I wanted to be sure that I had understood him correctly. "Janne?" I asked. "Is this about Janne?"

He shrugged his left shoulder.

"Well, as for me," said Friedrich from behind me, "I'm doing it a little for myself, too."

"My name is Friedrich and my body is disintegrating from within," said Friedrich into the camera that the guru held in front of his face. We sat on the lawn behind the family services center and watched. Only Janne had turned away and was bracing her head in her hands. Marlon was sitting on the grass next to her wheelchair and running his fingers along the wheels.

He had something that I never had before and would also never have. Something none of us had, least of all the guru. It wasn't coolness or what people identify as charisma. It was something that made you strain to hear his words because it seemed as if he knew a secret that he wasn't otherwise going to reveal. He didn't need Janne because plenty of healthy girls would chase after him on their two good legs. He didn't even know that Janne was attractive.

But *I* knew it. And 395 days ago I would have sat next to Janne and smiled at her. People always said I had a charming smile. I hated when they did; it sounded so dopey and innocuous. I had Lucy by my side and I was faithful to her, even if it was more out of laziness than true conviction. Except for the brief kissing episode with Johanna, the woman Frau Hermann sent to fill in for her once in a while when she herself occasionally needed to puke her guts out in a hospital bed—that's how Frau Hermann put it.

I heard my own teeth grinding.

Richard had detached his prosthesis and was doing something to his stump. I couldn't help but watch. The guru turned the camera away from Friedrich and pointed it at the detached leg laying on the grass.

"No," said Richard.

The guru lowered the camera. He hadn't expected it all to be so difficult.

"How did you find us anyway," I asked. "Did you use a specific strategy to get each of us here? Each one lured with something you thought would be interesting to us? Did you research our family and friends? Did we unknowingly pass some sort of casting process as particularly qualified cripples? Or is it all coincidence?"

"Coincidence is just the pseudonym God uses when he wishes to remain incognito," declared the guru with frustration as he covered the lens with a plastic lens cap.

"I've always wanted to learn how to throat sing," said Kevin. "I think it's unbelievably mean of you to trick me into this with false promises."

The guru looked as if he could live with it.

"What do you think of this," Marlon asked suddenly and sang a song I didn't know. I didn't even know what language it was in. Bright vowels held together by barely audible consonants wafted over my head. I felt dizzy. I lay back on the grass and closed my eyes. For a moment I forgot everything that had happened to me.

"I'm getting more and more yellow because my liver barely functions anymore," said Friedrich. "It's because of all the medications that I have to take."

"Poor thing," said the guru. "That's really a shame."

We were sitting on plastic chairs at a little round table. The guru had invited us to an ice cream parlor to try to lighten the atmosphere. It was the same one where I'd tried to shed a few tears.

The camera was rolling. It was pointed at the young woman in the black waiter's uniform as she balanced our ice cream bowls on a tray and tried to squeeze her way to the table between the legs of chairs and Janne's wheelchair. I leaned forward to hide my face. I was afraid she might drop the tray on my head otherwise. She kept her eyes trained on the ice cream and didn't notice anything until she had safely set down the last bowl on the wobbly table and then looked up.

I wondered whether the camera had captured everything. The interested glance at Marlon. The annoyed jealous look at Janne. The puzzled look at Richard. The disgusted look at Kevin and Friedrich, who was still talking nonstop about his innards.

And then the look at me.

She had no way of knowing I had been watching her the whole time. That behind my sunglasses I was looking directly into her suddenly wide eyes. She tripped over Janne's wheelchair and back to the counter. The others reached out their hands for their ice cream bowls and avoided looking at me. Even Janne stared into her ice cream with embarrassment.

"This could be a great film," said Richard after a pause. And then to me: "You'll be the star."

"I've already been the star once, thanks," I said.

Janne's face turned to me. For minutes on end, longer than ever before. I stared at my hands so as not to frighten her.

"What happened to the dog?" she asked.

"Shot," I said.

"And the owner went to jail?"

"No," I said. "He got a suspended sentence."

"And what have you been doing since then?"

"Nothing," I said. "I haven't been home for long."

"How long?" asked Marlon.

"Maybe half a year. Or a bit more. After the operations I was in a rehab center for a while."

"That's a long time," said Janne, running her hand pensively over her knee. She had very thin fingers. I wanted to touch her hand. She was probably cold. A ring would look beautiful on one of those long fingers, I thought, a heavy ring with a big stone, the kind Claudia liked to wear. Except they didn't suit her because she had short, fat fingers.

I imagined putting one of Claudia's rings onto Janne's finger.

"Do you play piano?" I asked.

She ignored the question.

"I play the flute," said Friedrich.

I have no idea why I rang my own doorbell. Maybe just to hear the shrill sound from outside. Nobody was there anyway. I had a key in my pocket; I'd been a latchkey kid since elementary school and it was something I was genuinely thankful to Claudia for.

The door opened and standing there was Johanna.

Life is full of coincidences, I thought ruefully. I had just been thinking about Johanna on the lawn earlier. And I hadn't thought of her for years. Now here she was in front of me. I pulled my hat further down my face and straightened my sunglasses.

"You've gotten so tall," she exhaled.

I let my gaze drop. "And you've gotten so pregnant."

She blushed. It looked as if she had swallowed a basketball. I looked farther down: her dress was short like back then, her kneesocks striped. She looked like an over-ripened Pippi Longstocking. She'd been studying something social-minded for years, if I remembered correctly.

"Can I come in?" I asked.

She stepped to the side. "It's your home after all."

"What are you doing here?"

"Frau Hermann's not well."

I managed for a moment to pry my gaze away from her belly.

"Is it serious?"

She didn't answer.

It was strange that today of all days I had remembered our tongues entwining. What could bring a woman in her early twenties to kiss a fifteen-year-old? I mean, sure, I came across as older, she'd said so herself afterwards. I had not forgotten the way she looked at me that time.

I pushed past her.

"How are you?" she asked my back.

"You can see for yourself."

"There's worse things," she mumbled. "You shouldn't get too worked up about it."

"Never. It's just a face."

For the next meeting the guru had asked us to come back to the meditation room at the family services center. This time he was punctual. We all were. Janne and Marlon were sitting there silently. Friedrich was chatting with Kevin about nightmares. Richard was reading the paper again.

The chair between him and Kevin was free.

"Hi, Marek," said Janne smiling. I nearly missed the chair and fell on the floor.

"Hi, Janne." My face tingled. Richard folded up his paper and looked at me for a long time.

"People, this isn't going to work," said the guru suddenly.

I had nearly forgotten he was there. He was sitting there on his chair, small and long-nosed and looking a little too distraught.

"I'm sorry, people," the guru said into the silence that had descended on the room.

"What?" asked Marlon.

"It was a stupid idea." The guru looked away as if to avoid Marlon's gaze, as if he had forgotten Marlon couldn't see anyway. "I'll give your parents the money back and we'll disband the group. It's just not going to work. I overestimated myself."

I thought of how I would go home with a hundred euros in my pocket. I didn't have to tell Claudia anything. She wouldn't know that I was no longer leaving the house every Thursday at three-thirty. I could go back to spending the entire day watching my fish and looking at images of deformed people in reference books without the annoying interruption. I would no longer be a participant in a self-help group for youths with physical and mental impairments. I could bid them all adieu with a light heart.

Especially Janne, who thought it beneath her to answer me.

Marlon sat there motionless. He probably loved to be filmed. I used to be photogenic once, too.

Friedrich's features were soft and his mouth trembled silently. Richard tugged at his earlobes, frowning. Kevin smiled pensively and looked at Marlon. And Janne . . .

Janne said loudly: "No!"

"What do you mean no?" The guru let his hat roll around on his knees the same way I sometimes did. "I say yes and I ask all of your pardon. You'll get your money back."

"Will you look for other disabled people?" asked Friedrich.

The guru waved his hand in the air. "You're not replaceable. It was doomed to fail from the start."

"No," repeated Janne.

She was sitting next to Marlon, very upright, and her green eyes seemed to be giving off sparks. I just couldn't get used to her face, it still surprised me every time. And even though there was as much space between her and Marlon as there was between Friedrich and me, I still saw them as together. And I thought to myself that there had never been a couple like that before, not in the movies or in real life. A couple that you had to congratulate on aesthetic grounds alone.

I suddenly had a bitter taste in my mouth. I would like to have spit on the floor.

"We're going to keep going," said Janne.

We're going to keep going, Janna had said.

Nobody asked her who she meant by *we*. Marlon and her? All of us? Since when were we a *we*? We had barely exchanged more than a few sentences with each other, we'd gone for ice cream together one single time, and we all made each other sick. I couldn't even figure out why I came back here and why the others did. Did they not have anything better to do, either? Were catfish and reference books the only things waiting at home for them, too?

And yet nobody disagreed with her. Not even me, even though I was suddenly very angry with Janne. I wanted her to look at me. I wanted her to smile at me. I wanted her to cry. Or do anything that showed she was a real person and not some alien trapped in the body of a cripple.

The guru was a bit speechless.

"I feel honored," he finally said, though it sounded like "you can all go to hell."

"Are any of you already eighteen?" he asked, looking around quite despairingly and lighting on me, oddly enough, as if my age hadn't been mentioned alongside my photo—the *before* photo—in every newspaper in the country.

Kevin slowly raised his hand. Nobody else.

The guru's eyes narrowed. The gears in his head seemed to clatter, as if he was trying to calculate something. "Okay," he said. "Minor mistake. Not even you, Marlon?"

Marlon leaned back in his chair silently.

"For now, it doesn't matter. Let's just get started," said Janne.

The guru said that if he was going to continue we would also have to make concessions. Meaning we had to show up on time, answer questions freely, and not bother our fellow participants. We had to be open, honest, and trusting. And in the end, together we would work out what united us despite all of our differences.

Janne sighed loudly.

"Have you ever done anything like this before?"

"Are we going down that road again?" asked the guru.

"Sorry."

"If you are referring to recording, then yes, I know how to hold a camera," said the guru huffily. "In another life, I even spent some time at film school."

"Probably as a janitor," I mumbled.

I have no idea whether Janne was listening to him or to me or to anything. Marlon's hand had just started to run along the wheel of her wheelchair again and we all looked away as if the two of them might start going at it right in front of us.

D irk's eyes practically jumped out of his head when I appeared at dinner in the kitchen on Wednesday. He was probably under the impression by then that Claudia locked me in my room all day and only let me out late at night, when everyone had sought shelter. I was wearing jeans and had ironed a white shirt. Just because.

"Shall I set the table?" I asked.

"That would be great," said Claudia standing at the stove with her back to me.

It smelled of garlic and some Indian spice. Claudia was turning lamb chops in a pan and the fat sizzled. Dirk sat there silent and pale.

For a moment I tried to put myself in Claudia's position. And I tried to imagine that Janne was there in Dirk's place. I broke out in a sweat. I wasn't sure whether to admire or pity Claudia now. Maybe it was a mistake to start mixing with people again tonight of all nights.

"Am I in the way?" I put large flat plates on the table.

"Don't be silly, we're happy to have you," Claudia answered mechanically. Dirk nodded in agreement several times.

Claudia carried the pan to the table, set it down, and kissed Dirk quickly on the cheek. I looked away.

They looked a bit ridiculous together. Given the chance, I realized I hadn't really looked carefully at Claudia in a long time. A few years before she had seemed noticeably more cheerful. Now, with her heavy eyelids and square chin, she reminded me of an ostrich. The lines in her face were really pronounced since she'd lost weight. Though she did have a super physique as a result. Her skirts seemed to keep getting shorter, and construction workers and taxi drivers regularly whistled at her well-toned legs.

"What happened there?" Claudia asked.

"Hm?"

She waved the spatula at my head.

"Johanna cut my hair," I said.

"Did you lose a bet?"

I felt the sides of my mouth tighten. But laughing still kind of hurt, especially when you tried not to. "I asked her to. So people wouldn't be so scared of me anymore."

"Nice," said Claudia flatly.

"Yeah, well," I said. "I actually think I would have been better off doing it myself."

She nodded and sat down. Dirk looked even younger sitting next to Claudia. His head was covered in light-colored fluff and as we ate I couldn't stop looking at his Adam's apple, which looked huge against his thin neck. With every mouthful it went up and down like a mouse struggling in a snake's throat. Since I had my sunglasses on I could stare at Dirk as much as I wanted.

"What is it you do again?" I asked.

He put his fork down on the edge of the plate and folded his hands. He was a lawyer like Claudia, he said.

"Where's your office? Do you have any chronic diseases? Are you married?" I asked.

To his credit, Dirk didn't turn to Claudia to look for help. He picked up his fork again and slowly sawed a piece of meat from the lamb chop as if there was nothing more important in the world.

"As a child I had eczema," he informed the bones on his plate. "I've heard you are interested in medicine?"

"I'm not the slightest bit interested in medicine," I said. "I'm interested in defects."

Just at that moment the phone rang.

I sat there like I was nailed down. It had been a family rule since I was little: never leave the table to answer the phone. Nobody rang these days anyway. Not for me at least. The answering machine clicked on. And then I heard Janne's voice asking me to call her back.

E xcuse me, please," I said to Claudia the next morning. I had set my alarm just to be able to apologize to her. Usually I didn't fall asleep until dawn, when I would gulp down a tablet, and then I didn't wake up until around noon. Dirk was already gone. The kitchen smelled like coffee and croissants that had been crisped in the oven. "I'm sorry about yesterday," I said.

"It's fine." Claudia kept reading the paper.

"I didn't mean to ruin it for you," I said. "Word of honor."

"If you could ruin something so quickly then it wouldn't have been worth anything to begin with," Claudia said as she continued to flip through the paper. She had on a gray skirt and a bright white top with a banded collar. The red polished toes of her bare feet felt around on the floor as if they were searching for fallen crumbs.

I sat down across from her, took a croissant from the bread basket, and broke off one of the ends. It was still warm. I dribbled a little lemon jelly from the knife into the open end of the croissant and shoved the entire thing into my mouth.

"Can I ask you something?" Claudia had put the paper to the side and glanced at me over the rims of her glasses.

"Yeah?" I asked with my mouth full.

"What's your plan?"

"For today?"

"Today, tomorrow. In general. Are things just going to go on like this?"

I didn't say anything.

"You had friends. You had interests. You did theater for god's sake. Was all of that so ephemeral that it just completely disappeared into thin air? Or can I assume that you're just taking a break and will get back to it all again at some point?"

I sighed, took a glass from the counter, made sure it was empty, and threw it onto the floor. Stupidly enough, it didn't break. Claudia didn't even glance at it.

"If you are so inclined to be destructive, then become a contract killer. At least it pays well."

I closed my eyes. I tried to picture it for a moment. How I would go to *his* house and knock at the door. How he'd open the door, looking just like an attack dog himself, an attack dog in human form, with his deformed hairless head, little murderous eyes, bared teeth. How I would kick in the door holding my weapon. How I'd give him time to recognize me before I pulled the trigger. How I'd smash the muzzle into the face of his girlfriend, who had laughed back then but was screaming in panic now. How I would let her live but she, like me, would never look the same again.

And then how I'd hear a baby crying in the next room and understand that I wouldn't feel any better and that I never would.

I opened my eyes. Claudia was reading the paper.

"I have no desire to live," I said.

"Oh, my god." She flipped the page.

"Look at me," I said. "Look at me right now for god's sake."

"I don't feel like it," said Claudia. "It's a horrid sight, men in their underpants at the breakfast table."

Only after I saw the taillights of Claudia's car out the window and was sure she wasn't coming back to get some files or her reading glasses did I call Janne back.

"Hello, this is Janne," she said, her voice warm and sunny, sounding every bit like a nice, carefree girl next door.

"It's Marek," I said. "Thanks for your call."

No idea why I said that. She had said basically nothing on the answering machine, and even if she had said something it was unlikely to have been something to be thankful for. I had an idea of what she wanted. She was worried that I was going to bail out. I had what it took to be the face of the project.

Together with her, of course.

Well, well, Marlon, I thought. You're blind and handsome. But I can use my face as a weapon. That counts for a bit more. Janne knows to appreciate it.

"What can I do for you, Janne?" I asked as dryly as possible. It was fun to say her name.

"Come over," said Janne.

"What for?"

"Pick me up. We can go to the meeting together."

Out of the question, I wanted to answer. Fifteen minutes later I was running out the door, combing my hair with my fingers, and noticing that it was unusually short despite the fact that I'd asked Johanna to go easy.

She lived in a white concrete box, the kind Claudia called a "townhouse." At the front gate was a sign forbidding dogs to shit there. Behind the fence colorful flowers with jagged petals bloomed. There was a fashion catalogue in the mailbox.

It was already too late when it occurred to me that I hadn't brought her anything. I was already here. I rang the bell.

It took a while before the door to the house opened and her mother waved to me from the doorway. The gate buzzed open. I walked along the artfully winding slate walkway past the flowers and across to the house. Janne's mother stared at me, a smile glued somewhat lopsidedly to her face. Her gaze skittered down me and landed on my hand, which I immediately stuck in my pocket.

"Janne," she whispered. "*The boy*. For you." And she quickly stepped to the side to let me in.

Janne's room was on the ground floor, naturally. She came toward me in her wheelchair. Close your mouth, I ordered myself. Now. I'd just told her mother my name and shaken her hand.

"Is Marek a Czech name?" she asked. She was still holding my hand, as if she wanted to show me that she wasn't the slightest bit disgusted by me.

"Slovak," I said. Janne rolled up to me and smiled. She had on one of her long dresses, this one in blue. She'd pulled her hair back in a ponytail. Her cheeks were flushed, like she'd just been exercising or was incredibly excited.

She reached out her hand. I let go of her mother's hand and touched Janne's fingers. They were cold, just like I had thought. I held them in my hand. I couldn't take my hand back because Janne was holding me tight.

"Come on."

I threw a smile at her mother that was meant to apologize and at the same time assure her that I didn't want to devour her daughter behind closed doors. The fact that Janne was still holding my hand was driving me crazy. Unlike her mother she seemed to be taking a perverse pleasure in it. Instead of enjoying it, I would rather have yelled at her: "What right do you have? What kind of game are you playing with me?"

Finally she let go and wheeled herself into her room ahead of me. It was exactly the way I'd imagined a girl's room would be. A pretty big bed, big enough for two people to sleep in, bookshelves, a big table with a gigantic monitor. I looked around for webcams. I spotted two right away. There was a white wooden wardrobe and its door was open, allowing a view of quite a few long dresses. On the dresser, which was also white, was a brush. Girls with no legs apparently arranged things no differently from the way girls with legs did. Janne closed the door and turned to me.

"When exactly did the whole thing with your face happen again?" she asked.

I was expecting all kinds of things, but not this.

"What's that question supposed to mean? Weren't you listening? Never seen a newspaper?"

"Is it true that you were really cute beforehand and that you were the star of your theater group?"

I shrugged my shoulders. It was clear she knew everything anyway. I just didn't understand why she was putting so much effort into getting a rise out of me.

"What do you want from me?" I asked. If she was going to get right to the point I couldn't see any reason I shouldn't as well. "Why did you invite me over, hold hands with me, and ask crazy questions?"

She leaned back and turned red. Bright red. It didn't suit her, not when she was normally so hard-nosed and unflinching and arrogant and unfriendly. When she blushed she looked like a little girl. A nice little girl.

I was immediately sorry for everything I'd said.

I sat down on the bed, on the floral patchwork bedspread, squinted my eyes so I could read the spines of the books on Janne's shelf.

"You get used to you," said Janne from the side.

I lifted my bottom and pulled out a pen that I'd sat on and was poking me.

"Now tell me about you," I said. "Since when have you been unable to walk, and where are your legs."

"Right here," she said with surprise.

I turned back to her. She was sitting perfectly straight, like a ballerina, and her cheeks were still slightly flushed. All of a sudden it occurred to me that not many boys could have been in this room before me, on this side of the webcam. Maybe the blind one. I closed my eyes to try to imagine how he experienced Janne's home. He probably had a really good nose but I couldn't smell anything except a hint of lime. I opened my eyes again.

"Where is *right here*?" I asked.

She grabbed the seam of her dress, that once again went down to the tips of her shoes, and lifted it up like a curtain.

I had pictured it completely differently. I'd assumed she had some kind of prosthetics like Richard. Or nothing, with the shoes as dummies. In any event I had not expected girls' legs, white legs stuck into even whiter socks. Janne lifted the skirt a bit higher and now I could see her knees.

"They look totally normal," I said. "Maybe a little thin, but otherwise . . . "

She laughed in a way that sent shivers down my spine.

"You can touch them," she said.

She didn't have to tell me twice. I slid off the bed and onto my knees. Janne bit her lower lip. Then I stopped paying attention to her face.

I put my hand on her calf. It was cool and somehow soft, like a stuffed animal. I ran my hand up and down. The skin was very smooth but there didn't seem to be any muscles beneath. But at the same time everything was beautiful. Just not really living. I didn't ask her whether she shaved despite the long dresses or whether her skin just didn't have the ability to grow hair. I hadn't come across that in the *Pschyrembel*, but I also hadn't read it all the way through. I moved closer and laid my head in Janne's lap, on the gathered cloth of her dress. I looked back up at her. She had thrown her head back oddly.

"I don't feel anything," she said, and her voice sounded different than usual.

I stood back up. Now I could look down at her. She had an unbelievable mouth, sensual and curvy. She wants to be kissed, I thought. There's nothing she wants more than that. I used to have a real life, but her? I didn't want to be envied by her for things I'd long since lost.

I leaned down toward her but she flinched backward.

The door opened. I hadn't heard her mother knock. Maybe she hadn't knocked. She was carrying a tray with delicate white teacups with gold rims and a matching teapot, and she put it down on Janne's bed. She looked me in the face with her eyes wide as if she was putting great effort into ignoring Janne's exposed legs.

"Or would you prefer coffee?"

I felt unbelievably sorry for her. Her life must have been

pretty hellish. Janne wouldn't have been easy to put up with even if she had functioning legs, but from her wheelchair she could turn anyone into a wreck in an instant.

Holding her hand was enough to put me on the verge of becoming a wreck.

"Are you also pleased with the group?" asked Janne's mother once she had found a point where she could focus her gaze: the orchid on the windowsill, which was so gorgeous that I would have taken it for plastic if not for the fallen petal lying next to the pot.

I didn't know how I should answer.

"Janne is like a new person since it started," said Janne's mother. "I'm really happy . . . I have to admit that I had my doubts. But he convinced me."

"Who?" asked Janne harshly, as if we didn't know the answer.

Janne's mother squinted.

"What did he tell you he had planned?" I asked as gently as possible because I felt bad for her.

"Didn't he tell you himself?" asked Janne's mother, confused.

Janne and I traded glances.

"Hinted at it," I mumbled.

"If we don't like it, we're going to quit," said Janne.

Her mother looked at her and shook her head. "I don't think that's possible," she said. "No, my dear girl, I really don't think so."

When her mother had shut the door behind her, Janne rolled over to me again. I couldn't understand why she had her eyes closed as she did, and wondered whether she planned to run me over and if you could get badly enough hurt by a wheelchair that you might need one yourself.

But when she coolly notified me that I was permitted to kiss her now if I still wanted to, I understood everything.

I didn't tell her that she was a dishonest, bored beast, that she was like a carnivorous plant lurking in wait for someone to come near it. I didn't say that I had no desire to be an extra roped into playing the lead role for her, or for her life, or for whatever else it was she had gotten into her head. I said nothing. I leaned down to her and kissed her on the mouth. She must have been pretty scared; she was shaking and her teeth, which I pushed apart with my tongue, were chattering a little.

Her lips tasted of fruit tea, the kind her mother had poured for us before she said those odd things. I thought of Lucy, the last girl I kissed before Janne. I hadn't wanted to see Lucy afterwards. And I was pretty sure I was doing both of us a favor, a much bigger favor to her than to me. Once in a while I'd clicked her Facebook profile before I'd deactivated my account, but in the meantime I'd avoided all the places we'd gone together, including the virtual ones.

I tried to remember what Lucy's mouth tasted like. Unlike Janne, she was a sweet-natured girl, nice and helpful and sunny, maybe not quite as pretty, but so much warmth emanated from her that I always found myself smiling for no reason when she was with me. She wanted to visit me in the hospital, but I hadn't let anyone in. In the months afterward, she still called and wrote me letters that ended at first with "kisses, Lucy" and later "with love" and then they stopped. I'd written her an email ending things with her in case there was anything left to end. I didn't get an answer to it and was both relieved and disappointed.

Janne had stopped shaking. My cheek tightened and this entire procedure was nothing like kissing used to be. I got angry. I grabbed Janne's shoulders and squeezed them. I had the feeling that if I didn't restrain myself I might crush her delicate bones with the palms of my hands. She threw her arms around my neck and squeezed the air out of me. She bit my upper lip. The last thing to bite me had been the Rottweiler. I grabbed her hair, which felt heavy and cool in my hand, and I wondered about the strange gasping and snarling I heard. Then I realized that it was us making those noises.

Suddenly she let go of me and rolled herself back a few feet. My knees were weak. I tensed them so they wouldn't buckle, suddenly consumed with the irrational fear that Janne had robbed me of the use of my legs and that from now on I was doubly cursed—no face, no legs. I braced myself against the wall and turned automatically toward the webcam. It seemed to be turned off, the red light wasn't on, so I didn't bother with a smile for the public. My legs were still there and they held me up. Janne watched me from a little distance with gleaming eyes and a very broad grin.

I pushed Janne's wheelchair across the sidewalk. Her mother stood in the doorway and watched us go. I turned and waved. She waved back, awkward and stiff. When I said good-bye she had kissed me on both cheeks and I breathed in her sweet perfume and blinked at the little wrinkles beneath the layers of makeup around her eyes.

I could no longer see Janne's face, only the part in her black hair. We didn't talk to each other. From up above I could see a bit of her lap, the depression in the folds of her dress, her small hands, her fingers interlaced.

"Should I get you a lapdog?" I asked while we were waiting at a traffic light.

"What for?"

"It would suit you. A yapping little pooch with a hair clip sitting in your lap."

"Great idea," said Janne.

It took us barely an hour to get to the family services center and that was only because I was so slow. I didn't go into the meditation room. This time we'd arranged to meet in the little garden behind the building. "So Janne doesn't have to go up any stairs," the guru had said. But there was a ramp at the main entrance or else Janne wouldn't have been able to get in the other times—I began to notice such things for the first time.

Everyone else was there, spread out on two wooden benches on either side of an old table which had a giant bottle of apple juice and a stack of plastic cups on it. They all looked at us, all of them, even Marlon with his sunglasses looked as if he was glaring at us. Now that we'd left the pavement it was much tougher to push the wheelchair. I started to sweat. The guru quickly hoisted the camera and pointed it at us like a weapon.

"Janne?" asked Marlon in a voice as taut as a guitar string.

" . . . and Marek," added Friedrich, beaming.

"Is that really the way to do it?" asked Richard after the guru had greeted us all. "Are you the team leader and camera-man all in one?"

"I'm everything, all in one." The guru walked around us with his device and I wanted to swat him away like a fly. "I always have been, my whole life. I'm the director, screenwriter, cameraman, speaker, cook, his girl Friday. A creator par excellence."

"Maybe we should fire you and get somebody else," said Janne. "Someone who understands what's up with us."

"Go right ahead," said the guru. "Why did you two show up together by the way? You're not starting something between you, are you? I'm warning you. Think of your children."

I choked on my apple juice. Everyone looked at me. Especially Marlon. I was sure that he did. Janne gazed into the distance with her hands folded in her lap as if she had nothing to do with any of this and least of all with me.

"Relationships," said the guru as if in a reverie, "are tough enough for us normal people. They could really drive you guys crazy. Does anyone here have a girlfriend? Does anyone want to tell us about it?"

Richard said nothing and without thinking began to fidget with the ring he wore on his pinkie. Marlon turned his face toward Janne and whistled a melody. Janne sat there like a bystander. And the poof named Kevin raised his hand and said, "I have a very sweet boyfriend."

But nobody wanted to know any more about that, so silence descended over the group again.

"People, this isn't going to work," said the guru after a pause.

"Exactly," said Janne. "We're wasting our time. You need to do your work or there's no point to all of this."

The guru closed his eyes. Then he opened them again and exhaled slowly, like a boy who has just accidentally climbed up to the ten-meter diving platform. "There's no way to avoid it," said the guru. "We have to take a trip. All of us, together."

W hat's this?" asked Claudia when I put the note on the table.

"You have to sign it," I said. "Right here." I pointed with my finger.

She straightened her glasses and leaned over the piece of paper. "You're going on a trip with your group?"

That sentence was like a punch to the gut. Total self-destruction. Yes, I'm going on a trip with my group.

"You?" asked Claudia skeptically. "*You are going on a trip with your self-help group?* Why am I just learning about this now?"

"Everything is explained there," I said. "It's a spur-of-the-moment group decision. You said yourself that I should socialize more."

"I said that?" Claudia read the sheet of paper through for the fifth time. "I'm not signing this until I've spoken to him."

"Please don't. I've already been humiliated enough."

Claudia shook her head. Then with a flourish she signed her name on the space that was separated from the informational letter by a dotted line and a tiny scissor symbol.

"But a thousand euros for one week," she said, "that's a heck of a lot, my dear. Weeklong camps run by the school cost a fifth of that. How do you like the guy who runs it anyway?"

I ignored her question. "It's because the accommodations are handicapped accessible."

We ate the three of us again that evening. Dirk had given up trying to engage me in conversation. He twisted his spaghetti onto his fork and chatted with Claudia about scuba diving. I liked him a lot better this way. I twisted my spaghetti on my fork and looked through a travel book on Mecklenburg-Vorpommern.

Until Claudia took it from me, shut it, and tossed it onto the chair next to her.

"Pull yourself together," she said.

"I'm going away for a week with my self-help group," I said to Dirk as if in confidence. He was wearing an unbelievably pink shirt. I'd heard that even men wore pink these days, but it bothered me on him.

"Really?" he asked politely. "Where are you going?"

"Marenitz," I said.

"And where is that again?"

I didn't know myself. The guru said something about a three-story villa. A room for him, a room for Janne, three double rooms for "you guys," kitchen, and a common room with a woodstove. I knew it was going to be a disaster and I knew I would definitely go anyway.

"Will you look after Claudia and feed my fish during my absence?"

"Certainly."

"That eases my mind," I lied.

I was lying in bed and looking at the catfish in the aquarium when Claudia knocked at my door.

"Phone for you," she said and was already in my room before I said "come in." She handed me the phone. "You're very much in demand lately. It's almost like the old days."

I took the warm phone out of her hand. An anxious, frail female voice vibrated in my ear canal. I quickly scratched my ear because it tickled. And that's how long it took me to recognize the voice of Janne's mother.

"I just really wanted to know if you were also going on this trip, Marek," she said. "It makes me nervous to agree to this scheme since I don't know anyone. Except for . . . " Her voice trailed off again.

I was so surprised that all I could do was cough. And then I said yes to everything. Yes, I will look out for Janne. Yes, I'll hover around her. Yes, I realize she has limited mobility. Yes, I'm prepared to come by so she can tell me all of this in person and shake my hand one more time.

She hung up and I felt like a pantry moth on flypaper.

She was standing in the doorway again, waiting for me. She was very slender, that's what I noticed first. In her slim-cut dark blue pants and white blouse with round collar, she could have passed for a girl, from the back at least, a girl from a previous era, maybe the thirties or the fifties, I couldn't have told you the difference.

It seemed to me that her smile was a bit less tense than it was the first time. That was normal. People got used to me.

"Marek." Again as a greeting she held my hand in her ice-cold fingers. "We've been expecting you."

And I thought, why in the hell didn't you bring flowers, you idiot? If not for corrosive Janne then at least for her mother.

As I went down the cool hallway I wondered whose voices I was hearing floating toward me from the slightly open door. One was clearly Janne's, but the second one? Of course I recognized it instantly and just pretended I didn't, because the knowledge of whose voice it was gave me a pain in my stomach that transformed into nausea. I knocked a little too loudly on the door. On Janne's bed sat a smiling Marlon, and Janne was laughing so much that I was tempted to take her for a cheerful twin sister. When I'd been there recently she hadn't laughed like that. Actually she hadn't laughed at all.

They greeted me with a bland cheerfulness, like a married couple who patiently accept being interrupted by the mailman in the middle of the most fascinating conversation. I leaned against the door and tried to control my breathing. What I really wanted to do was run away, hurt and insulted. But I didn't want Janne to laugh at me. I would like to have killed the last woman who laughed at me. But the only one who was killed, other than me, was the Rottweiler.

I noticed a red rattan chair in the corner and sat down in it. My behind sank deep into the seat cushion. Janne smiled. To what no-doubt-important rationale did I owe the honor of my invitation, I asked her loudly.

"Mama wanted it," said Janne casually. "She's all worried about the trip."

I would have done exactly the same thing if I were her mother. I just didn't know what her worries had to do with me. I asked Janne, in the hopes that she'd be embarrassed that her mother had dragged me into it despite the fact that she, Janne, was busily devoting her time to another guy.

"Mama just wanted to meet the other people going on the trip," said Janne as if it went without saying. She certainly didn't look embarrassed. "That way she'll be a little more comfortable with it. I've never gone away on my own before. Without Mama."

"And why are you now?"

"Because I want to."

Then she forgot me for a while and began chattering away again about some meaningless claptrap. It had been a long time since I'd been so thoroughly ignored. I couldn't remember if I ever had been. When she got around to talking about breeds of dogs, I got up and left the room without a word. That is, I wanted to leave the room but ran into Janne's mother in the doorway. She invited us all to the dining room for tea.

We sat at an oval table. The tablecloth was hanging way down on one side. I was next to Janne's mama, Janne next to Marlon. Behind us a piano, on it some open sheet music.

Her mother poured fruit tea and pushed the milk and sugar

around the table like they were action figures. I had the impression that she was putting real effort into making sure she divided her attention evenly between me and Marlon. You couldn't say the same about Janne. She just kept talking about dogs.

I turned to Janne's mother and asked her what she did. She was a translator from Swedish and French. I reported that I had a Slavic name; I completely forgot that we'd already talked about that during my first visit. I said I also had a Ukrainian stepmother who wasn't much older than me. She'd been our au pair.

Not much older than me wasn't entirely accurate. Tamara had been eighteen then, and that was already seven years ago.

Janne's mother fell sheepishly silent. I'd always thought that the mothers of disabled children wouldn't be easily shocked. But maybe her husband had run off with an au pair girl as well. In any event, she didn't want to delve any deeper into the subject of my stepmother, so I asked as politely as possible what she was working on at the moment. She was translating a book on suicide, she said, and the writing was very intense. I praised the topic and revealed to her that my mother was a divorce attorney.

"Right," she said distractedly, "I've heard about her." I discovered time and time again that a lot of people had heard of Claudia. Clearly the institution of marriage wasn't in great shape.

I finished my tea and got up. Janne and her mother both came to the door to say goodbye. Janne's mother said she was happy that Janne would be accompanied on the trip by such wonderful young men, that it would be almost like family. She sounded suspiciously like the guru but I generously ignored that fact. I told her I'd like to read one of her translations, if the one about suicide wasn't finished then another one about a comparable topic. Janne shook my hand and forced me to bend down so she could give me a kiss on each cheek. Little devils danced in her eyes. I suddenly understood why someone might want to strangle a girl he was in love with.

I desperately tried to convince Claudia not to drive me to the train station. I said my bag wasn't heavy at all and that I could find the correct platform on my own. If any complications came up I could always ask somebody (at that point I pushed my sunglasses up on top of my head for a moment and Dirk flinched). Claudia said in an annoyed tone that she didn't have to go all the way to the platform, but that she at least wanted to drive me to the station, she owed that to me, to herself, and to our, she paused briefly, group leader. He's the last person she owed anything, I said. He's an asshole and a liar, but on the plus side there's a pretty girl going. Claudia started to cough and I rapped on her back.

Dirk piped up that he could do it, too. Take me to the station. I wondered what made him think he would be any more palatable to me as a chaperone than Claudia was. Then it became clear that he suspected I didn't like feeling controlled by Claudia.

"Sure, you drive me to the station," I generously permitted him. "My mother is always busy at the office at that time of day anyway."

It was more complicated than I expected.

The night before, I'd already thrown everything into my suitcase, including six pairs of sunglasses in identical leather cases, when the phone rang. I figured it was Janne again or at least her mother wanting to reassure herself that I really would keep an eye out for Janne. But I was disappointed. It was Kevin on the phone, and he asked me in a friendly tone how I was planning to get to the station.

Like an idiot I told him the truth. He asked whether it would be too much trouble for us to pick him up. He lived practically around the corner and his boyfriend had to go to work. He gave me a street name I'd never heard of before. I didn't really have any choice.

Claudia said goodbye with a kiss on the cheek and a slap on the back—like I had dust on my back. I promised to send her a text as soon as I arrived. Then she was off, and I stared at the spot where she had just been standing.

Dirk drove a two-seater convertible. There was a backseat, but it wouldn't have held anyone bigger than a munchkin and our gang of cripples didn't include one of those. I squeezed my suitcase into the tiny trunk. Kevin would have to tie his to the back, I thought, and it would roll along behind us.

"We have to accompany a fellow traveler," I said formally.

Dirk nodded, hemmed and hawed a bit, and finally asked what kind of disability the person had.

"I don't know what you would call it," I said. "He's crazy. Apparently he went after somebody because he heard voices. And he's also a poof; I don't know how the two things are related."

From that point on Dirk didn't say anything more.

Kevin didn't live anywhere near me but rather over at Gesundbrunnen, on the third floor of a yellow-painted concrete high-rise block. He waved out the window and something about his dark profile disturbed me. The door buzzed open even though I wasn't planning to go upstairs. Dirk left the car in the middle of the street with the motor running and came up the stairs behind me. It obviously made him a little uncomfortable. He must have loved Claudia a whole lot given the things he did for her. An early version of approval germinated inside me.

My forebodings were confirmed as soon as I entered the apartment. Kevin had lined up several small bags in the hall, each decorated with a pearly luggage tag. Unfortunately he himself was completely naked.

"Are you not ready?" I yelled. "Do you think the train will wait for you?"

"I'm ready," said Kevin.

I picked a T-shirt up from the floor and tossed it to him.

"Not that one," he moaned, but then he glanced at me and back at the shirt and threw it on. Then, nearly unprompted, he set off searching for a pair of pants. I looked into the kitchen, which was small but spotless. I couldn't wrap my head around the fact that Kevin supposedly lived here with a partner. At the end of the day I still felt like Claudia's little mama's boy—I'd only just learned how to run the washing machine. Yet I was only a little younger than Kevin.

"I'm ready," Kevin repeated proudly. I nodded: this time he had jeans on. They were cut off just below the knee and a fringe hung playfully down.

I grabbed two bags, Kevin the other three. Dirk, whom I'd forgotten in the staircase, mumbled something about making himself useful. Kevin had just closed the door when he suddenly screamed shrilly.

"What now?!?" I shouted.

"I forgot," he moaned, "I forgot about Kongo."

He pulled a key, hanging on a cord around his neck, out from under his T-shirt, bent over, and unlocked the door without taking the cord off this neck. He raced inside; I followed him yelling threateningly. Kevin ran into the kitchen, snapped up from the floor a bowl filled with sticky jam-filled cookies, and emptied it into a waiting bag that was already half-full of the same cookies. Then he shook fresh ones into the bowl from a box and stood up smiling.

"Kongo smashes everything to bits if he doesn't get fed."

"Is Kongo a cat?" I asked weakly.

Kevin shook his head.

"A dog?"

Again he shook his head. I decided I didn't really want to know.

"One last question, what's that stuff?" I pointed to the bag where he'd just dumped the cookies that had already been in the bowl.

"Oh that," said Kevin. "Kongo already ate that."

At that point I just shut down.

The only ones who'd been accompanied to the station by their parents were Janne and Friedrich. Janne's mother was talking to the guru. Even at a distance I could see that the guru was sweating. Instead of his usual hat he had on a baseball cap that out of nervousness he kept taking off. He was probably hoping right to the end that none of us would show up.

Friedrich's father towered over everyone. His gray hair gleamed like a helmet on his head, and with his crest and his graying mustache he looked like an aged Hitler Youth member. I would never have taken this man for Friedrich's father if Friedrich hadn't fought his way over to me and introduced me to the Hitler-grandpa, whom he addressed as Papa.

Friedrich's papa looked at me and not a single muscle moved in his ruggedly creased face. He shook my hand with a very firm grip but unlike Friedrich didn't say much. Actually nothing at all. Together with Janne he was the second person in a short period of time who didn't deem me worthy of a second glance. Maybe he used to work at a clinic for burn victims or as a military doctor. But then he would have done something about the basal cell carcinoma spreading across the left side of his forehead. Though maybe he wanted a natural death rather than having medications screw around with things.

The guru stood on his tiptoes and counted us. In an attack

of generosity I had allowed Dirk to come with me to the platform after we'd dug Kevin out from under all his bags in the backseat. First and foremost because Dirk also wheeled my suitcase. He was also carrying some of Kevin's luggage and it made him look unbearably gay to me. Kevin stumbled along behind with a smile on his face that seemed directed at nothing concrete and at the same time at everything.

Dirk's gaze went from one person to the next, taking in the prosthetic, skipping over Friedrich, and paused quizzically on Marlon. And then it arrived at Janne. I saw how Dirk exhaled and I suddenly felt jealous. The way he gawked at her bothered me.

"Thanks a lot and *auf wiedersehen*," I shook his hand stiffly before he hit on the idea to hug me.

"My pleasure," he said. Suddenly I felt bad for him.

"Take good care of Claudia and feed my fish, Dirk," I said.

He nodded, turned quickly, and left.

During boarding there was some confusion concerning Janne. The guru had informed the rail authority about the guest with limited mobility. Now two beefy men in uniform had assembled in front of her, and Janne looked at them in such a way that left them afraid to do anything. Janne's mother stood next to her and red splotches appeared on her cheeks.

"We've never traveled by train before," she said as I went over to her.

Janne's face twisted into a grimace. I was afraid she would start to cry. As supremely self-assured as she normally was, that's how shatteringly helpless she now seemed. And before I knew what to do, Richard shoved past me. He squatted in front of Janne and asked her something quietly. She nodded and rubbed her eyes with the back of her hand. Richard planted his feet, bent down, and effortlessly lifted Janne. She reclined in his arms like Snow White being taken out of her glass coffin. Friedrich's father fiddled with the wheelchair in the meantime. It clicked and then the wheelchair was suddenly totally flat and looked quite light.

"Here," said Hitler-grandpa, shoving it into my hands.

Nope, it wasn't as light as it looked. I had a tough time holding it with one hand. I looked at my suitcase. Janne's mother pulled it to the door for me. Janne's voice came from up above us. She waved happily out of the open train window.

"Hurry, hurry," the guru urged, and I got the wheelchair into the train and jumped back down to grab my suitcase.

With nothing to do, the uniformed station attendants carried Kevin's bags aboard. I turned around. Marlon was standing on the platform as impassive as a Coke machine. Nobody seemed to have thought of the fact that he might also need help. His duffel bag lay at his feet.

For a second the thought shot through my mind that we could depart without him and he wouldn't say a word, he'd just be left standing there. I reached for my suitcase with one hand and for Marlon's elbow with the other. "Here's the door," I said.

He put his arm out and his fingers clenched my shoulder. His grip was strong and for a moment I panicked, thinking he might break my collarbone. The guru yelled from the railcar and Janne's mother hurried over and grabbed my suitcase again.

"Quickly, quickly," she said. I wondered whether she was really worried about us or only about Janne. Maybe she had realized what wonderful young people she had entrusted her precious daughter to.

I took my suitcase from her and climbed onto the train with Marlon in tow. "Watch it, steps," I said too late, when Marlon was already cursing and had let go of me for a second. Janne's mother hoisted Marlon's fallen duffel bag. I turned around: apparently she was trying to decide whether she dared to give Marlon a push from behind. Luckily she decided against it.

We stood panting in the railcar and the door snapped shut in our faces. I waved to Janne's mother. Her smile was pained and relieved at the same time. She crumpled a tissue in her hand. Friedrich's Hitler-grandpa went over to her quickly, taking broad strides, and patted her elbow. Then the platform disappeared from view.

I pushed open the door to the compartment. It was already full. Janne was sitting next to Richard. Friedrich and Kevin had taken the seats opposite her. The last free seats had luggage on them. Janne looked at us and I could see in her eyes that she would like to have swapped us for some of the people sitting near her. But maybe it was only Marlon she wanted to swap in.

He was lucky he hadn't seen how easily Richard had lifted Janne on the platform. After I had such difficulty handling the wheelchair, I looked at Richard differently. And it was clear that Janne must have as well. There's no way I could have lifted a girl up and into a train with my own two legs. I looked skeptically at Richard's upper arm, but there wasn't much to see under his loose-fitting checkered sleeves.

She probably didn't weigh much, I decided. Maybe her legs didn't weigh anything. Legs must make up a significant portion of a person's weight. I just needed to exercise a bit more and I'd be able to carry her.

The guru waved from the next compartment.

Marlon stood there like a statue that someone had accidently unveiled in the wrong place. His face didn't show any emotion. I said to him, "It's full here. The guru is waving to us from the next compartment," so he wouldn't wonder why we still hadn't sat down and were just standing around like idiots. I wondered how Marlon got around the city and whether he ever went to areas he didn't know. Maybe a cane or a dog would really have come in handy. I'd had all sorts of impressions of Marlon—but that he was helpless had never occurred to me.

We sat down with the guru after I stowed my suitcase and Marlon's duffel bag on the luggage rack. It suddenly hit me that I was the least impaired person in the group. Though I was still the ugliest.

The guru had put his cap in his lap and was flipping through a stack of documents. Between nondescript slips of paper were ticket printouts and entire sheets of handwritten notes. I craned my neck because I thought I recognized Claudia's handwriting on one of the sheets.

The guru had two deep lines running across his forehead. His face was flushed.

"Problem?" I asked. Marlon sat casually next to me, facing the window as if watching the landscape fly past.

The guru shrugged his shoulders. "Depends on how you see it."

"Where's the camera?" I asked.

"What camera? Oh." He pointed to a blue bag in the luggage rack.

"May I?"

He obviously didn't have the slightest desire to give me his camera, but he stood up anyway and reached for the bag and pulled the camera out with both hands and handed it to me. I turned it all around. It looked cheap.

"Can you really work with something like this?" I asked. "Can you make a real movie on it?"

"Of course," said the guru without looking up at me. "Should I show you how it works?"

"I can figure it out," I said, testing a few buttons.

Marlon still hadn't moved. I turned on the camera, started recording, and pointed the lens at Marlon. No idea what he picked up on but all of a sudden he said, "I'm going to punch you in the face." He'll have to find my face first, I thought, somewhere in his perpetual darkness, but I didn't say it. I also didn't say that I could have left him standing there on the platform earlier. I took the camera out into the hall and started shooting the little gardens passing by.

They were laughing in the other compartment. I couldn't understand it. In our compartment the atmosphere was like a funeral and here they were laughing like they were on a school field trip. I pointed the camera at the door to the compartment. They had drawn the curtain. No chance to get a candid shot. I felt locked out and knocked on the door.

The laughing stopped. I pushed open the door and pulled

the curtain aside. Friedrich's chuckles were the last to die down. They looked at me as if I was the ghost of their dead aunt. I looked at them through the viewfinder. They were playing cards. A bag of gummi bears was being passed around.

I pointed the camera at Janne. She was shuffling the cards and looking at her hands as she did. I had the impression that she was trembling slightly. Maybe it was just the vibrations of the old train. Her wheelchair was folded up and propped between the seat bench and the door.

"You guys are having fun, eh?" I asked in a funereal tone and filmed as guilty looks spread across their faces.

There were fewer and fewer buildings and people outside. I stood in the corridor and filmed the birch trees racing past and the long lakes. The guru turned up next to me and took the camera away.

"The battery doesn't last forever," he said.

He stood next to me and leaned on the handrail exactly the same way I was. I didn't look at him. I felt like getting out at the next station and hopping on the next train back to Berlin. These local trains stopped in the most godforsaken places. The isolated figures who got on at those places looked somehow deformed. As if I of all people could complain about that. Behind me bubbled Janne's laughter. I would really like to have taken a machine gun to the whole scene, and I wasn't even embarrassed by that thought. I should have learned a lesson from Marlon: disgraced down to the last bone in his body and yet still cool.

"This week is going to change lives," said the guru from next to me.

To be honest I wasn't the slightest bit interested what the guru hoped to gain from this week. But I still asked, "Yours or ours?"

"Both," he said.

I tried not to smile too broadly. "Inflated expectations have never helped anyone."

"I'm a little bit scared," said the guru.

"Of what?" I stifled a yawn. "Of us? It's too late for that."

He exhaled loudly and looked really depressed as he did.

"It could still end up being some interesting footage," I said with a sudden flash of sympathy.

He nodded again. His face betrayed the fact that he was assuming the opposite would be true.

Getting off the train, unlike getting on it, went pretty smoothly. Taking a cue from Richard, we had formed a line in the corridor in advance. Everyone listened to him, and the guru seemed grateful that somebody who was up to the job was taking over the steering wheel. Friedrich carried Janne's wheelchair and looked really proud. The guru shouldered Friedrich and Marlon's luggage in addition to his own.

Marlon's hand was on my upper arm again. I could barely stand it. I hated being touched. The sudden solidarity of our disabled troop made me want to escape. All for one and one for all. I didn't want that. Not with these people or anyone else. I was already sick of it.

In no time at all we had lined up on one of the two platforms of the tiny little station. The only thing missing was for us to be put into pairs and told to hold our line buddy's hand. The guru counted heads. Sweat dripped from his forehead. Friedrich opened the wheelchair as if he had been doing it his entire life. Janne smiled down at us from Richard's arms. The sun shone.

It turned out we had about a twenty minute walk to our lodgings. The guru had arranged transportation for the luggage but he didn't seem to believe that it would come. We were waiting outside, sitting on our suitcases, when a tractor rattled into the parking lot pulling a trailer. At the giant steering wheel was a boy who couldn't have been older than twelve and next to him was a shaggy bear-sized dog. The two parties looked at each other curiously for a while until the guru realized this was the transportation to the farm.

We threw our bags into the trailer and the tractor chugged off. We walked around the station building and found a paved path that curled into the woods. The guru compared something on one of his sheets of paper with the sign at the start of the path and turned on the navigation function of his phone.

"I can take a turn," I said to Richard, who had stationed himself behind Janne's wheelchair. He nodded indifferently and stood aside for me.

"Did you ask me?" asked Janne with an unpleasantly high-pitched voice.

"May I, Janne?"

She ground her teeth together. I took this as a yes. After the first few meters I was already bathed in sweat and began to suspect that Janne's mother didn't need to go to the gym to keep herself so fit.

The promised twenty minutes stretched on for an eternity. The paved path gave way to a gravel path and then a dirt path. At some point I realized we'd been walking for nearly an hour. Nobody said a word, Kevin just hummed a tune. He moved like a stork on his stilt-like heels, swinging his bag back and forth, and he didn't seem the slightest bit bothered that the ends of his heels kept sticking in the sandy soil. The guru was a few meters ahead and had been on the phone for the last ten minutes.

"I'm hungry, I'm hungry," Friedrich repeated as if in a trance.

"Then eat some grass," said Marlon.

Those must have been the first word I'd heard from him all day. He had finally let go of me and was walking with light, tentative steps in the middle of the group. I kept waiting for him to bump into someone but it didn't happen. Now and then he made a strange clicking noise with his tongue.

"I saw somebody do that on TV but I couldn't figure out how they did it," said Friedrich enthusiastically.

Marlon didn't think to enlighten him.

When I was sure that we were lost the guru suddenly put his phone in his pocket, and gestured with his arms.

"We're here!" he yelled. From where we were there was still nothing to see but trees. The guru waited until we caught up. And when we did, I wasn't the only one who stood there with my mouth wide open.

I was prepared for all sorts of things. That we would be staying in a horse stall or in a yurt or in dilapidated tents. The last thing I expected was a forest villa with towers that reached up to the clouds. A yard spread out in front of the house, and behind it was some kind of shed with a grill and a nicely stacked pile of wood. Our bags were stacked at the base of the stairs that led to the entrance.

"There must be another way here," said Friedrich profoundly, fishing out his suitcase and backpack.

I just stood there, still gripping the handles of Janne's wheelchair. Even she had turned her face up to look at the towers. The guru climbed the stairs and reached under the doormat.

"By the way, there's a ramp!" he called to us and then stood up again. He raised his hand proudly into the air; in it gleamed a key.

I sat down on the bed and untied my sneakers. Against the opposite wall was a second bed. Marlon was lying in it with his arms crossed on his chest. He still had his sunglasses on so I couldn't say whether he was sleeping. His breathing was soft and steady.

We were so close that there I was listening to his breathing. I didn't like it. This handicapped accessible villa was certainly big enough for each of us to have a separate room. I got the feeling that the sleeping arrangements were part of the plan, and I was an opponent of such a plan.

The room was spacious, with a huge antique chandelier hanging from a ceiling that must have been three meters high. There was a giant window that Marlon found immediately and threw open. The light white curtains fluttered in the breeze and I felt like I was in an Impressionist painting. The chest looked antique. Near the window stood a secretary, and I looked to no avail for a inkwell on it. It was a giant, fantastic room, but stuck in there with Marlon I felt confined.

To take my mind off it I tried to imagine what I must seem like to Marlon. Probably an amorphous sweating, panting, heat-radiating lump.

"Why are you lying there like a corpse?" I asked.

He didn't answer. I didn't expect him to. I had an idea of what was going on with him. He too had imagined everything differently. He had wrongly assessed both himself and the trip, and he felt humiliated about looking helplessness in front of Janne. So he had as much right as I did to hate everything here, myself included.

I opened the well-oiled door to the room, went out, and closed it quietly behind me.

The guru was unloading boxes of groceries that some-one had obviously left for us in the kitchen. He looked a bit more relaxed. Across the polished counter rolled apples and lemons while the smell of mari-nated meats and olives wafted out of bags, and I would love to have just bitten right into the big loaf of dark bread sitting on the table.

"Why don't we have our own rooms?" I asked with the slightly annoyed tone of a package tourist. "There seems to be more than enough space."

"Because they are renovating," said the guru without turn-ing around.

"So who'll be doing the cooking?" I didn't think there would be anything wrong with my taking a banana. After all, Claudia had paid for the groceries.

"You."

I decided to take it as a joke, left him to sort out the gro-ceries, and moved on.

The villa had a wheelchair-accessible elevator between the ground floor and the second floor. I took the wide staircase with the wine-colored banister that had been polished by many hands. Upstairs, where our room also was, I found half a dozen doors. Some were locked. I heard Kevin giggling behind one of them. He was sharing a room with Friedrich. I wondered whether the guru was going to room with Richard or whether an exception to the plan would be made in this particular case.

And I wondered why others always got luckier with such things than I did.

Janne, of course, wasn't upstairs. I went back down the steps, my hand again sliding on the now-warmed wood of the banister. I'd last seen her just after our arrival as she disappeared behind the door to her assigned room on the ground floor. The guru carried her suitcase in after her.

I knocked on the door.

She answered, sounding cheerful and welcoming. With a vague sense of gratification that she was feeling at ease, I turned the doorknob. Janne's wheelchair was in front of the wardrobe and she was sorting her things. Girls, I thought. I never would have thought to unpack the week's worth of clothes I had.

"Can I help?" I asked.

She nodded.

I took a hanger off the rod and handed it to her. She put it into the neck of one of her dresses, smoothed it out, and gave it back to me. I hung it up. So it went, until, after the seventh dress, I couldn't restrain myself any longer.

"How long are planning to stay here? Or are you going to change before every meal?"

"You have a problem with that?"

Eventually we emptied the suitcase. I looked at the hanging dresses with their lace and flowers and puffy sleeves. It looked like the costume closet at my old theater group that Lucy had taken care of. She was handy at it. We sure were a committed group back then. Oddly enough, Lucy didn't mind at all staying behind the scenes and taking the old clothes home to wash and iron, all of which she had found at secondhand shops and flea markets. Her name didn't even make the program, and neither did the names of many others who, I now realized, worked a lot harder than I did to make our shows possible. And my face was on every ticket. Mustn't they all have hated me?

"You fit in pretty well in a place like this," I said.

Janne smiled, flattered.

I sat down on the bed without asking. Without the web-cams she must have felt like something was missing. The guru's dilettantish handheld camera was surely no substitute. There was a dresser with a mirror next to the window, there was a brush and other girlie stuff on it. Suddenly I felt emotional. I reached out my hand and tried to catch Janne's fingers as she rolled past me.

"Do you like me?" she asked, looking me in the eyes.

I turned away. Her gaze was as sharp as a knife. A frilly, flowery razor blade.

"You are very pretty," I said. I would've loved to have said something that would have surprised her a bit.

I wanted to kiss her again. If I was honest, that was exactly the reason I was here. The only reason and at the same time the most pressing reason. I wanted to kiss Janne. I didn't need to do anything else for the whole week. Maybe even for my whole life.

I pulled her close.

She lifted an eyebrow, her arm tensed. She gave me a look that was both skeptical and coquettish, as if she didn't want to make it too easy for me. That was certainly not the way you looked at someone you were scared of. But then again there probably weren't many people she was scared of.

All this thinking was taxing my brain. I didn't want to think anymore. In the hospital, with all the bandages that had made me into a mummy, I didn't have much else to do but think. So I'd laid there and my thoughts had swirled until I got dizzy. Sometimes I tried to quiet them with music or an audiobook, but my thoughts were always louder than whatever I put on. Nothing had ever tested me like that before.

I tilted my head and shook it, as if the memories might fall out of my ear, then I leaned over to Janne and kissed her. She turned away and I grazed the tip of her nose and a little of her cheek, delicate and covered with an invisible fluff. Her skin tasted more bitter than it had the first time. But she smelled of limes once again, fresh and fragile like a flower that was so delicate it was threatened if you so much as breathed on it. She pushed me away and hid her face.

"Is that why you came?" she asked.

"It's not why you came?"

I thought she was going to be mean now but she just laughed.

"Where is Marlon anyway?" she asked.

No, anything but that! It was the one sentence that could not have been said at this moment. I gasped for air.

"What do you want with him? He can't even see you."

She glared at me contemptuously. It was the kind of look that should have frightened me. The fear I saw in other people's eyes was nothing compared to this.

"Tell him that I want to see him. If it's no bother. And now piss off."

"Good evening to you as well." I slammed the door behind me.

Obviously I didn't say anything to Marlon. I wasn't Mother Teresa. I let him continue to relax in our shared room in the pensive pose of a corpse at a public viewing. Our *shared* room—just thinking of that made my stomach churn. I probably couldn't have stood to share a room even with Janne.

"Spoiled only child," stated the guru with the knowing and overly-kind smile that I had learned to hate. He was looking at his camera, checking out the footage he'd already shot, but he hid the display from me. I had sought him out to complain again. What I would have really liked to do was to take the camera away and make everything better. I'd long since realized what a dilettante he must have been. If the others didn't get it, that was their problem.

He pointed the camera at me.

"Yes, I'm a spoiled only child," I said into the lens but hadn't even finished saying it before it occurred to me that it was factually inaccurate. Technically I wasn't an only child. I had a little brother.

I'd never seen him except in photos that Claudia showed me years ago. A naked baby stumbled around in the pictures. I had refused to tolerate any of it. I wanted nothing to do with the baby because I didn't want anything to do with my father, either, who'd had a heart full of love for our au pair and balls full of speedy sperm that destroyed my peaceful only-child existence forever.

My father came to Berlin a few times, supposedly to meet up with me. I figured he must have just had business meetings there. For Claudia's sake I went with him once to the zoo and once to the natural history museum. We'd sat on a park bench and eaten ice cream, which even then didn't taste very good to me, and he wanted to show me a picture of this other boy whose father he had become. I had asked him why he was sitting there with me if he had another son. Having more than one son at the same time seemed absurd to me. He coughed oddly and then took a big bite of his ice cream cone. It must have hurt his teeth given the way he had grimaced.

Later on he wrote me a letter and for my birthday and Christmas sent me first Legos and later money. I didn't answer the letter because I was too polite to write the things I really thought. I accepted the gifts.

Then came the Rottweiler. Claudia told me that my father had come to the hospital immediately. Once. It had been hard for him, Claudia said.

"I'm a spoiled only child," I repeated. But the guru was already walking down the stairs with the camera.

The guru had been bluffing. On the first night, he cooked. Veal cutlets wrapped in bacon, green beans, baked potatoes, and for dessert homemade panna cotta with raspberry sauce. I was so hungry that I nearly choked as I greedily wolfed down the delicacies. My stomach was cramping up.

"You should be a chef," I said to the guru. "This is your true calling."

He looked across the table at me with sad dachshund eyes.

I had seated myself between Friedrich and Richard. Janne was across from me. Although she seemed to be eating the whole time, the amount of food on her plate never actually diminished. We'd waited forever for this dinner and had basically not had anything else all day. When Friedrich had tried to complain about it the guru had answered that he should walk to the nearest grocery store and get himself something. Friedrich looked out at the woods with his eyes squinting skeptically. When nobody was willing to go with him, he stayed in the villa and bugged everyone with his grumbling stomach.

"Do you always eat so much?" Richard asked Friedrich over my head.

Friedrich shook his head. "Usually more."

I took a second helping and thought with a full mouth that the guru wasn't such a bad guy. Something was off about him, something major, but you could say that about almost everyone these days. With a full belly it was tough to concentrate on what a pain the coming week would be. I almost began to look forward to it.

Until my gaze fell on Marlon. He was sitting next to Janne. She had asked him to take the spot next to her as soon as he'd shown up. Me on the other hand she had not asked. He had only just then finally—and heroically—rousted himself from bed. Now he was sitting next to her and guiding small bites into his mouth with his fork while I waited for him to spill something on himself.

I tried to look at them in a relaxed, benevolent way, and was successful until Janne stroked Marlon's arm and whispered something in his ear.

I'd had enough at that point. I threw my fork onto the table. It fell clattering to the floor.

"What's the plan for the week?" asked Kevin.

"Do we have one?" asked Marlon, and I could see how Janne's warm breath tousled his hair.

While the guru, still wearing his chef's apron, explained the various outings to the churches and cow stalls of the area, I stood up and picked the camera up from the counter. I turned it on and walked around the table. I wanted to do it for Janne, so she could continue to think that she'd come out of this a star, or at least come out of her YouTube ghetto. If it made her so happy to have people look at her.

The truth is, I found it fun to shoot video. I zoomed in on the plates. On Friedrich's greasy glistening lips. On Janne's hand, which had wandered into the crook of Marlon's arm. Looking through the display I no longer saw it as something that drove me crazy but rather as a thrilling visual motif. I zoomed in on Janne's full plate. She'd eaten only the beans and cut off a tiny piece of her veal cutlet. It was the only plate that wasn't eaten completely clean.

She's anorexic on top of it all, I thought. Then I zoomed in on her fingers playing with Marlon's arm, and my compassion had reached its limit.

I was so engrossed that I totally missed the guru's lecture on what our collective purpose was here. I watched Janne's face in the display. And it was clear as day that she didn't like the sound of the plans. She wanted to stay at the villa. The guru said, no problem, then the others would be the only ones on camera.

Bull's-eye.

I pointed the camera at the guru's face. I zoomed in to get the little wrinkles around his eyes. He was older than I had first thought, and no longer as frantic as at the start. But he still didn't look exactly relaxed, more like a nervous, tattered teddy bear. His lips were closed tightly and the corners of his mouth drooped. It wouldn't have surprised me if he was just gone one morning and we found out that the rent for the villa had not been paid and all our valuables were gone.

I turned off the camera and sat down again at my place at the table. The platter of potatoes was empty. So was the pan with the veal. Friedrich, I thought angrily, and looked across the table at Janne's plate.

"Are you finished with that? Can I have it?"

She pushed it across to me without looking at me. I ate it

with her fork, which was still on her plate, and looked at her the whole time, until she shook her head contemptuously.

"What?" I asked.

"Nothing. You're so young and yet already such an asshole."

That summed things up perfectly.

There was a wood fireplace in the house but no dishwasher. So it fell to Friedrich to build a fire and to me to wash the dishes. We both protested, but the guru acted like a dictator and wouldn't discuss it. He untied his apron and handed it to me. I took it and threw it on the table. Then I set up in front of the sink.

"It's been ten years since I washed a dish by hand."

"Then it's about time." He watched as Friedrich put a big, round log into the fireplace and pulled a long match out of the pack. It hissed, then broke off, and Friedrich dropped the box of matches and the long matchsticks went all over the floor.

I wasn't sure if I would have done any better, which is why I didn't laugh.

I let hot water run into the sink and dribbled in dish soap. Marlon was still sitting at the table. It was almost as if he wanted to watch me. The guru clicked his tongue in commiseration as Friedrich screwed up his fifth attempt to light a match and shoved a dish towel into Marlon's hand.

"Help Marek dry the dishes."

To my surprise, Marlon didn't object. He came over and stood next to me, too near in fact, and I moved over a little. I put dripping wet dishes into his hand. He dried them and stacked them on the counter. The guru documented the cooperation between Blind and Deformed.

I dunked my hand into the warm foamy water and watched as Richard went over to the fireplace with a few sticks and a piece of paper. He pushed aside the nearly-sobbing Friedrich, kneeled down, and stacked the twigs into a sort of tent. Soon enough flames were dancing behind the glass doors, which Richard wiped clean with a damp cloth.

"Nicely done, Richard," called the guru, and you could clearly hear the former kindergarten teacher in him. "Don't worry about it, Friedrich."

Richard gave him an annoyed look and the guru fell silent, embarrassed. Then suddenly a smile spread across Richard's face. Behind me I heard the sound of Janne's wheels on the wood floor.

"Are you cold?" asked Richard standing up to let Janne get close to the fire. She shook her head but did pull closer to the fire and stared at the flames. If she had stared at a lake the same way I would have grabbed her to keep her from jumping in. The guru turned the camera around. She straightened her shoulders and pushed a lock of black hair from her forehead.

Marlon had heard her, too. His whole body had tensed. I had the feeling he was vibrating.

"Will it take you much longer?" Janne asked him as if he were all alone.

He can't see how much is left, I nearly said. Though he had probably been counting the plates. What did I know about how he perceived the world. What did any of us know about each other.

"We're done," we said simultaneously.

"Have you seen my room yet?" Janne asked Marlon. "Would you like to?"

"Yes," answered Marlon, and then it got so quiet that we could hear the fire crackling.

I didn't get a wink of sleep that night. I thrashed around in bed, threw off the covers, picked them up off the floor, opened the window, closed it again. I barely managed to sit still for ten minutes. My heart felt as if it were beating in my throat and threatened to stay there. I turned to the wall so I wouldn't have to look at Marlon's empty bed. The bedspread with the lemons and parrots was still on it, the pillow was still indented in the shape of the back of Marlon's head.

Marlon was with Janne. The whole night. I forbid myself to leave the room and creep around the villa. To put my ear to Janne's door. To storm in there and smash everything to bits. A few times I couldn't hold back the tears and I cried for a couple minutes like a wounded animal—until I stuffed a corner of the blanket in my mouth. Outside it was quiet and I felt like the last human being on earth.

Marlon's bag sat there still unpacked next to his bed. On his nightstand was an iPod with headphones. I couldn't think of anything better than to throw it out the window. It smacked with a dull sound into the flowerbed.

An hour later I felt bad. I pulled on my pants and slipped out of my room. To get out I had to go past Janne's room. The floor creaked under my feet. It was silent all around. Everyone but me was asleep.

I carefully pushed open the heavy entrance door but couldn't keep it from closing behind me with a dull thud. I crawled around the roses beneath my window but couldn't find the iPod. I looked everywhere, it was just gone. I laid down on the lawn and stretched out all four of my limbs. The grass was moist and the cold crept under my skin. I closed my eyes.

And opened them when the door closed again. On the steps stood Richard in tight sweatpants and a tank top. It was suddenly light out, too light out. I must have fallen asleep. I quickly shielded my face with my hands. Richard looked at me at that same moment. His legs, aside from his prosthetic, were knotted ropes of muscle. His long hair was held back with a headband.

"What time is it?" I asked from the lawn.

"Six-thirty." He waved and set off. I struggled to my feet and stumbled up the steps.

The next person I saw was Kevin. His friendly face with the lurid lipstick was looking down at me.

"Don't growl, it's only me. Breeeeeaaaakfast," he sang melodically and pulled on my blanket. I grabbed it, too, and held it on me. I didn't want to be naked in front of him.

"Ten o'clock," said Kevin. "Everyone's waiting."

He stood next to the bed, nodded his head, and looked at me as if he would only leave the room together with me. I pulled the covers up to my chin.

"Get out."

"You're welcome." He stomped out, hurt.

I leaned my head over the edge of the bed and looked at the floor, where my dew-soaked clothes were lying. Then I looked at Marlon's bed. There was a damp towel there now. His bag was still in the same spot but the zipper was open.

He'd been there, I thought, grinding my teeth. He'd showered and seen me sleeping.

Bullshit, he can't see.

My head felt so heavy that I just wanted to fall back onto

my pillow. My eyes felt like somebody had poured half a sand-box in them. I closed them and imagined my fist smacking Marlon's face. I licked my lips, and suddenly they tasted salty.

They were indeed sitting around the table, which was already set. They were all in a better mood than I'd ever seen. The guru was telling a joke that I only caught the end of, and there was simply nothing funny about it. The camera was nowhere to be seen. Kevin was standing at the stove frying eggs, sunny-side up. The place smelled of butter and burnt wood.

I straightened the sunglasses on my nose. They were all sitting in the same places they had yesterday. Janne was wearing a white dress and her black, still slightly wet hair fell to her shoulders. She didn't look up when I came in. She was distracted. Marlon was leaning down to her and whispering something in her ear, and she nodded and laughed. I shoved my balled fist in the pocket of my pants.

"What happened to you?" the guru asked cheerfully. "Sleep poorly?"

"Slept great." I poured myself a glass of orange juice.

"I found an iPod in front of the building, who does is it belong to?" The guru held up the little silver device.

"Marlon," I said as everyone looked at the stupid thing blankly.

"How did it get there?" The guru put the iPod on the table in front of Marlon. Marlon silently slipped it into his pocket.

The plan for today was to go someplace together. The guru said he wasn't there to lug groceries around for six big guys— or rather five big guys and one lady. We needed to decide what we wanted to make and then go shopping for the ingredients together and bring it all home. Who wanted to go first?

Kevin was the only one who spoke up.

I drank the juice, which sat uncomfortably in my cramped stomach, and studied Janne and Marlon. I wanted to know whether their faces had changed since yesterday. If they themselves had changed. I devoured them with my eyes. I wondered whether the marks on Marlon's face were the imprint of Janne's pillow. I wondered why the guru was permitting this Sodom and Gomorrah. Whether he even noticed what was going on here. Whether Janne's mother would think it was cool that Janne was in such demand here that she could pick out her companion for the night.

I was ready to deploy the entire arsenal of weapons so as not to see Marlon next to Janne. Nothing was verboten: I would have no problem tattling on him, denouncing him, or physically hurting him. I felt like I wasn't even me anymore but rather the Rottweiler, capable only of drooling and biting.

"Stop eating," I said to Friedrich, who was spreading a third roll with butter, cream cheese, and jam.

"Go fuck yourself," answered Friedrich. I was so surprised I didn't know how to respond. Even Janne stopped massaging Marlon under the table for a second and turned her almond-shaped eyes on us.

"Good morning, Marek," she said, as if she had just realized I was there.

Good morning, roller-slut was on the tip of my tongue. And that was the nicest description of her that occurred to me. I hardly recognized myself anymore. I hadn't felt so attacked since the Rottweiler.

I carved up a piece of bacon just to have something to do. I wasn't hungry anymore. The others had already stood up and headed off in various directions. Friedrich shuffled over to the sink with his shoulders slumped.

Marlon was standing at the top of the stairs with a hand on the bannister. I thought about how much I had enjoyed the feeling of the bannister's smooth wood yesterday. Now he had his hand on exactly the same spot. I never wanted anyone to touch anything that meant something to me, ever again. I got up and went up the stairs toward Marlon and ripped off my sunglasses so I could see him better. Marlon turned his head toward me before I even tapped him on the shoulder.

"Can she feel anything at all?" I asked. "Down below, I mean?"

Everything went quiet behind me. Marlon turned his whole body to me. Then he put a hand on my shoulder, practically hugging me. His other hand he put on my head. I realized too late that he was just finding his bearings with that hand. His punch hit me right in the middle of my face and took me off my feet. I lost my balance and fell down the steps.

It was a little bit like the other time but also completely different. Once again I had no face and I pressed my hand, which hadn't been able to protect me, to my face—only this time there was no animal attached to it. There where my face had been was now a raw schnitzel. No upstanding person would ever think to mutilate a good cut of meat like that. It hurt, but the pain felt strange, like it wasn't a part of me. And anyway I didn't generally have much of a problem with pain anymore. These days I could put my hand right on a burner and not even realize I'd charred my fingertips. Maybe back then I'd gotten an overdose of pain medication that was going to last for the rest of my life.

"Take your hands away from your face," I heard Richard's voice. "It's not like it could get much worse anyway."

When I didn't budge, somebody tugged on my wrists. I kicked and—I was happy to feel—caught something soft and squishy. Moans of several different pitches rang out.

I have wanted to scream. They said I screamed back then. I didn't want to know the details—I would never have attributed the high-pitched, unmanly sound that rang in my ears to this day with myself. I felt their eyes on me, on the backs of my hands, the good one as well as the mangled one, on that which my hands could never really hide, just as the sunglasses couldn't, either. I felt more naked than naked, like they had skinned me to see what I looked like underneath. I swung both elbows and hit someone else, someone solid. Then I sensed a moist, burning touch on the sides of my hands and I growled.

"I'm just wiping off the blood," said Richard.

"Can you move?" To judge by the sound of his voice, the guru had already shat himself.

The question interested me. My face wasn't the only thing that hurt. So did everything from my neck down. That was also a big difference from back then. The Rottweiler had also knocked me over, and I had hit the back of my head and my ass. But it didn't really play much of a role. Now for the first time I discovered I had a spine, and I wasn't sure I could still use it. I was suddenly aware of my shoulder blades and hipbones in a way that I didn't like.

"Not sure," I answered the guru. My voice sounded strange. I felt bad for the guru. If I ended up a quadriplegic he would be in some seriously deep water.

"Did someone get that on film?" I asked.

The cold washcloth slapped at my face again. I shoved it aside, fought gravity, and sat up with a groan. Something fell into my lap. I felt for the sunglasses and put them on and then opened my eyes.

The first thing I saw was the face of the guru. In it I saw nothing but pure, distilled relief: like somebody had promised him a share of the winnings from a lottery ticket and then changed their mind, and then in the end they had paid him after all. Obviously he was of the opinion that somebody who could sit up on his own wasn't badly injured. I basically believed the same thing. Richard reached toward my face unprompted and straightened my glasses. Now I saw it, too: one lens was broken.

I looked into the distance through the cracked glass. Janne was nowhere to be seen. Marlon was standing off to the side. The others were all kneeling around me and the shock, mixed with a dash of morbid curiosity, slowly spread across their faces. The guru looked as if he had just stepped in dog shit.

"What the hell is with you guys?" yelled the guru out of the blue, with his chin swinging back and forth between me and Marlon. Obviously he wasn't worried about my bones anymore. "Have you lost your minds? Beating each other up, and on the stairs of all places? Do you have shit for brains?"

"It's all my fault," I said before Marlon could open his mouth. "It won't happen again."

"I guarantee that. I'm calling your mother." The guru tried to stand up. He had been squatting down too long, his legs must have fallen asleep, and the feigned sadness in his voice sounded tense. "That's it. I'm terribly sorry for you, Marek."

I staggered to my feet and was able to verify that I could indeed stand. My skull was humming again and my knees felt treacherously weak, but even so it felt better to be standing than to be lying there like a bearskin rug at their feet.

"Don't even think about it," I said.

The guru opted for extortion. Either I had to be examined by a doctor or he would inform my mother and let her decide whether I could stay or not. Even though prior to the fall I wanted nothing more than to get the hell out of there, now I was going to fight it tooth and nail.

"Doctor it is then," the guru concluded.

The nearest one was in the village. His name and phone number were posted in big letters all over the villa. The guru went off to find a spot where he had phone reception so he could call the farmer and pay him to use his trailer as a medical transport.

"I'm coming, too," said Marlon all of a sudden.

"No!" said the guru and I simultaneously, and then I thought: why not, actually?

"It's okay with me," I corrected myself.

The guru wasn't so easily convinced. Apparently nobody had figured out why Marlon had knocked me on my ass. But everyone seemed convinced that he must have had good reason to do it. Nobody suggested, and nobody threatened, that he should be sent home.

"I can go, too," said Richard.

"Really?" The relief in the guru's voice sounded almost obscene. "Then I can stay here with the others. Don't want them to beat each other to a pulp as well." He playfully wagged his finger at Janne, who had just appeared on the horizon, as if she had nothing to do with all of this.

Before the farmer showed up, I went into our room. I took off the bloodstained T-shirt and left it to soak in cold water in the sink. I turned my back to the mirror and took off my broken glasses, tossed them in the wastebasket, and grabbed a new pair from my suitcase. I felt around my face with my fingertips. Some spots were swollen and felt more numb than the rest. There were probably bruises there. There must have been a scratch above my right eyelid that was dripping blood into my eye. I wet a washcloth and cleaned everything up as much as possible. Then I contorted myself to try to feel my spine.

The door opened and closed again. I turned around. Marlon was there with his ear turned toward me.

"I'm here," I said.

"I know."

"How?"

"You're snuffling like a hippo. The faucet is dripping and you just turned it off. Also you're shifting from one foot to the other."

I stopped shifting.

"You're an idiot," he said.

"What a novel way to apologize."

"You don't deserve an apology." Marlon spoke slowly and seemed to stretch the words as if he was saying something that didn't need to be said. But with someone as stupid as me, well, he'd just have to spoon-feed it to me, obviously. "I didn't realize you were standing right at the edge of the stairs and that I could have killed you, but I swear, if I had known, I would have done exactly the same thing."

"Because of Janne . . . " I started to say.

"Not because of Janne. Because of you. Because you're such an idiot."

I wished I could have disagreed, but he wasn't finished. And besides, we heard the tractor rumble up the house and suddenly we were both in a hurry to get out and we ran into each other in the doorway.

He pulled his elbow away when I went to support him, and he walked a few steps ahead of me on the stairs, holding the bannister.

We sat silently in the trailer as we trundled down the asphalt path passing sheep and cows. It would have been faster to walk. I couldn't continue the conversation with Marlon because Richard was sitting across from us whistling away. The things on the tip of my tongue were intended only for Marlon and me.

So nobody said anything and that was fine with me. Up front in the tractor sat the same boy and next to him the same shaggy dog. We jerked and bounced along and every time I knocked against the side of the trailer it felt like a bolt of lightning shooting through my entire body.

"I really don't think I need a doctor," I said, finally breaking the silence.

"A kick in the ass is what you need," said Richard.

After a good two hours the tractor came to a halt in front of a general practitioner's office in an old timbered house. I felt like a cocktail. As I got out I tried not to spill any of my contents but refused Richard's helping hand. Marlon hopped down and smiled nastily when he heard me groaning.

"Next time I'll throw *you* down the stairs," I whispered.

He laughed out loud. I wanted to kick him and could easily have done so. But I didn't.

In the waiting room sat two old men in dirty overalls, both with canes. It smelled like cow shit. They broke off their conversation as we came in, eyeballed us for several minutes, and then continued talking. I didn't understand a word.

The doctor, a fairly young, chubby man, pushed on the purple blotches, turned my head to the left and right, and shined a little lamp in my eyes. He had obviously been forewarned about my face. Richard had insisted on coming into the doctor's office with me, he didn't trust me as far as he could throw me. The doctor said I had no broken bones, just contusions and bruises and perhaps a mild concussion. He would be happy to stitch up the wound on my eyebrow, not for medical reasons but rather on aesthetic grounds. I looked at him skeptically. He didn't bat an eyelash.

"It's fine as is," I said. "Very nice of you."

He let me leave only after he gave me several prescriptions for cooling, anti-swelling, and pain reducing salves. The nearest pharmacy was in the next village and the boy with the tractor was gone. I threw the prescriptions in the wastebasket at the deserted bus stop.

"I told you guys I was okay," I said to Marlon and Richard.

"Do you even have anything in there to concuss?" said Richard, pointing at my head. I could have answered and even knew what I would say. But I didn't say anything. I wondered silently why everybody was suddenly picking on me. They hadn't even found as much fault in Friedrich. I mean, I hadn't planned on becoming everybody's darling here, but this was the first time I'd ever been treated as an enemy of society who needed to be constantly monitored.

We went back by foot. It didn't take half as long as it had by tractor. Marlon was between us, he clicked his tongue now and then and he stumbled just one time. Once again we didn't speak to each other.

The others had set up a circle of chairs on the lawn with an empty spot for Janne's wheelchair. The guru was writing feverishly in his notebook. Friedrich was talking. The camera was nowhere to be seen.

Everything's back to normal, I thought. All good.

My injuries weren't life threatening, Richard answered the question in the guru's eyes and then went over to the shed to get more chairs. The guru ran his hand over his forehead.

"You're back quickly." He had probably been looking forward to having an entire afternoon to recover from us.

"You look terrible," Kevin said to me, shielding his eyes with his hand. "I can't look."

Oddly enough, I was touched. Even though I'd only been away a few hours, I was happy to see them all again. They also seemed happy that I was alive and hadn't ruined their week by dying a silly death. We were a big, happy family in which one brother beat the other up, but at the end of the day it was done out of affection.

The sister was the only one who sat there with her face averted, ruining the joy of the reunion.

We joined the circle of chairs, which widened to accommodate us.

"I don't know what's going to happen moving forward," Friedrich continued. "The eventual outcome of my clinical profile is multiple organ failure, just like my two uncles on my father's side."

Marlon sighed loudly. Friedrich fell silent, unsettled.

"But you go to a regular school?" asked the guru, who seemed to remember he was conducting a sort of interview that we had interrupted.

"I try," said Friedrich. "Whenever I'm not out sick or being treated at the hospital."

"I'm really, really afraid of hospitals," Kevin said. "Especially when you can't open the doors from inside."

I turned to him so as not to continue staring at Janne's lap, at the creases in her dress. Oddly enough, I liked Kevin in a way that I myself most likely confused with sympathy. Kevin looked like he wasn't going to do well for much longer. Like something terrible was going to happen. And then I would feel sorry for him. Because he was the nicest queen I'd ever met. Of course, he was the only one I'd ever met. In the last 436 days I had basically seen nobody.

"And you, Janne," said the guru, "what are you afraid of?"

I was sure that she wouldn't answer. But she turned to him and said, "Stupid questions."

"Do I ask stupid questions?" asked the guru in an understanding tone.

"They're fine," said Janne generously. "The worst ones are the questions people don't say out loud, the ones written on their foreheads. What happened to you, cutie? Wouldn't everything be easier if you were at least a little uglier? Can anyone love you the way you are?"

My heart beat so hard that I could hear the echo in the back of my head. Boom, boom, boom.

"You're totally sweet, of course everyone loves you," said Kevin.

Instead of jumping for his face with claws extended, she looked at him gratefully. Apparently she liked him, too. But I wasn't so insanely jealous of him.

"When I was little I went to the elementary school around

the corner from our house," she said. "I was the special needs kid in an immersion class and there was an extra assistant there to help me. And all the children thought I was just pretending. That I could hop around just fine and was just too lazy to walk on my own."

"Maybe you shouldn't have told them you were a princess under a magic spell," said Marlon.

Janne turned to him. Suddenly I realized that the whole punch and collapse had been completely unnecessary. Nobody was ahead in this race. Janne hated him no less than she did me.

"And then what happened?"

"After the fifth grade I stayed home and only went to the school to sit for exams."

"That worked?" asked Richard. "I mean, that's not against the rules? Don't you have to go to school?"

"Yes, you do," said Janne. "But not in my case."

"Did you get a certificate that said you were impaired?" asked Kevin eagerly.

Janne smiled at him. "How did you know that?"

The guru put down his pen and leaned forward. "What I wouldn't have given for a certificate like that when I was your age."

And suddenly it came pouring out of everyone. It was loud and it was weird; it was laughter. Even Janne giggled, and on Marlon's face I saw a trace of a smile. I was the only one who didn't laugh. I was shocked. They were joking around with each other like old friends enjoying their time together. They were happy about trivialities and about the fact that I hadn't broken my neck. They had forgotten that we were just a bunch of cripples and head cases. I was the only one who still knew it. Again I was filled with a sense of foreboding.

We had to go into town again because there was nothing left of the groceries bought the day before. Apparently the others had killed the time without us by eating. The guru said that we could have thought to go shopping after we went to the doctor's office. He probably had already forgotten how he was so worried about me—or perhaps about himself—that he wanted to call Claudia and have her pick me up. I asked how we were supposed to know what was needed. The guru shook his head.

"Like little children. You have to cut everything up and spoon it into their mouths."

Dumbfounded by these sudden expectations, we watched as he walked frantically around the grill, which was in front of the shed. Earlier it had been sunny, but now it was noticeably cooler and the air was crisp. "We need charcoal, bread, meat, vegetables," the guru enumerated while rubbing down the grill with a napkin. Then he spun around and screamed without warning, "What are you waiting for?"

Kevin went inside to freshen up before the shopping trip. I tried to explain that for me personally, one trip a day to the village was more than enough. Marlon was nowhere to be seen. And then Janne suddenly said she definitely wanted to go.

Because of Janne we couldn't take the shortcut through the woods. We had to take the longer, paved path. I pushed her wheelchair with her silent acquiescence and I didn't let on that because of the fall my back was wrenched and the pain was spreading down my leg. Now and then I stopped and tried swinging my hips to get rid of the pain. I could have stripped naked while doing it, nobody was paying the slightest attention to me. Janne was chatting away with Kevin about the right technique for creating smoky eyes. At first I thought they were making fun of somebody but then I realized they were actually deadly serious about the topic. I didn't have much to contribute.

When we set off, the guru had stood on the stairs with the camera and filmed our departure, as if he wanted to remind us that we were assembled here for a higher purpose.

Kevin said his boyfriend was an actor. I saw how Janne's back immediately straightened.

"What has he been in?" Something about her voice sounded different.

"TV shows."

"And how does he put up with you?"

I could hardly believe my ears, that she would ask that. It seemed like a mix of tactlessness and stupidity. After all, I never asked her: "So Janne, what's it like being in a wheelchair, what do the boys in the neighborhood make of it?"

Kevin wasn't insulted.

"No idea," he answered. "I can't possibly explain how he puts up with me."

"He probably loves you," said Janne sadly.

"No idea," Kevin repeated, smiling broadly. "He's a bit older."

I killed the time by looking down at Janne's neck. Her hair was clipped up in a bun. She looked like she was from another century. Her skin was delicate pink and unbelievably vulnerable. I never would have thought that you could kill an hour staring at a girl's neck without getting bored. But I actually had no desire to ever do anything else again. One black lock of hair had fallen out of the clip, I stared at it and could have cried.

In the village I treated Janne to the experience of being in the company of someone who enjoyed a certain notoriety. Apparently my visit to the doctor's office had made the rounds. There were more people out and about than earlier in the day and their eyes popped out of their heads. It was tough to tell whether it was because of me or Janne. Or because of Kevin and his high heels, his pink cap, and handbag that he swung back and forth by its long strap. Probably a combination of all of us.

In the little grocery store we realized that Janne's wheelchair wouldn't fit through an aisle because it was full of cartons. I was going to steer to another aisle but Kevin stopped me. He put his handbag in Janne's lap and began to move the boxes out of the way. He lifted them up and stacked them in another aisle, next to a pallet of mustard jars.

"It's fine," whispered Janne, turning bright red. Even her neck, which I could see from behind, was covered with red splotches. Now I felt really sorry for her, I could feel her embarrassment in physical form, I could grip it in my hands. Then I roused myself out of my stupor and started to help Kevin. Some of the boxes I just threw behind Janne, figuring we didn't have to go back by the same aisle.

A short-legged man in the blue uniform of the store hurried over to us.

"Put everything back immediately," he cried in a high voice that, combined with his mustache, created cognitive dissonance. Even Kevin's voice was lower, at least when he wasn't trying to speak in an artificially chirpy voice.

"We can't get through here." Kevin handed one of the boxes to the man and smiled innocently with his lipstick-covered mouth. "We're here, as you can see, with a wheelchair."

The man took the carton and held it to his chest for a second before putting it down, befuddled.

"You can run riot at home," he said, and his unbearably high voice made my teeth hurt.

"We're not running riot." Kevin maintained his sweet temper. "We're trying to get through."

"Get out!" yelled the store manager suddenly. Janne cringed. I moved a box aside with my foot so I could get past the wheelchair and make sure she wasn't about to cry. For the first time, I entered the foreground in the store manager's field of vision. Apparently up to that moment I hadn't stood. He gasped nearly silently, stumbled backwards, and tripped on one of the moved boxes and fell onto his back. With his feet he kicked a pallet of cans. That's when things got loud and messy.

I SIMPLY CAN'T BELIEVE IT!!!" I never would have thought the guru could shout like that. He screamed like he was at a soccer stadium. His spit flew in every direction, I cowered so it wouldn't hit me in the face.

"Psst," said Kevin calmly. "The police are listening."

"THE POLICE?"

We hadn't yet left the station, but the guru had already blown a gasket. I thought he was overdoing it. Or to put it another way, I could certainly understand that his nerves were shot after this first day, but I was aware of nothing I'd done wrong in this case, and the same was true of Kevin and Janne. We tried to explain but he didn't want to hear it.

"Get out the camera," said Janne when the guru stopped shouting.

"WHAT?!" He lost it again for a moment.

"The camera. You have to film this. The way we're being arrested. Wrongly, just because we're handicapped. This is amazing stuff, really."

"Not arrested, detained," I corrected.

The guru squinted his eyes.

"I feel sorry for your mothers." But he pulled the camera out of the blue bag that was hanging from his shoulder.

"Film us coming out of here," said Janne.

Kevin picked his handbag off the floor and held it up. I got behind the wheelchair. The guru held the camera. At that moment a police officer popped out of a side door and asked about our filming permit, shouted that we'd already caused enough trouble, and threw us out.

"Are we going to have to appear in court?" asked Kevin, scratching his nose. Once we left the police station the guru wanted to go by himself into the supermarket where the manager had called the police to get us arrested for disturbing the peace. We would have to wait outside, which we didn't mind at all.

"I don't think we'll have to go to court," I said. "Any trial, if they even initiate one, would get shut down fast. No supermarket chain can afford to look so hostile to disabled people these days."

"We'll have to hope that's true," said the guru darkly.

"Our pride should keep us from shopping here," said Kevin.

"If there was another store in this dump," snapped the guru before storming into the grocery store. I suspected he wasn't pissed off only because of the police but also because his plan to grill was threatening to fall apart. But that wasn't our fault. There was only one butcher in the village and it closed up at noon. The refrigerator section at the supermarket had just two packages of pork sausages left on offer. The view of those sausages seemed to put the guru over the edge. We could see him through the glass front of the store, standing there in the aisle, and I was afraid he might break down in tears, too. Finally Kevin ignored our ban from the store and went in, and a little while later they emerged carrying heavy bags of groceries.

Aside from the ten pathetic sausages, we grilled corn on the cob and sweet peppers, wrapped in foil and buttered and salted. It was all Kevin's idea, including the lentil salad and tabouli. It all tasted great, and Kevin was pleased by the compliments until I asked whether he really liked to cook or was just a picture-perfect queer. No idea why he got so pissed off.

I f anything more happens, we're cancelling this whole thing," slurred the guru. There'd been five bottles of red wine in the shopping bags. Kevin had poured a little for each of us, but now all five bottles were empty. "If anyone else falls down the stairs or starts beating each other up, or if I get even the slightest hint that you're not all in your own rooms at night, or if you cause trouble and I have to bail you out of the police station, then you're all packing your bags right away!" He tried to pound his fist on the picnic table but he lost his balance. Marlon, who was sitting next to him, caught him.

"I'll be in the shit if anything happens to you guys," blubbered the guru after he'd freed himself from Marlon's grasp and laid down under the bench to, as he put it, feel the earth. "So many children and I wasn't able to be there for them, and you guys aren't kids anymore and you still don't have a clue. You're already crippled, it wouldn't take much. A slight breeze and you're done for. It's probably all my fault."

Kevin, who had also hoisted more than a glass, also started to cry. He slumped to the ground and laid his head in Janne's lap. I tried not to step on the guru in the dark, and looked quizzically over at Marlon. I hadn't given up hope that he might actually still meet my gaze at some point.

Richard gathered up paper plates that had fallen on the ground and stacked them on the table. Four skinny cats emerged from the darkness. They sat next to each other on the edge of the lawn, aiming their shiny eyes at us and meowing.

Janne fished a cube of cheese out of the salad and tossed it to them. They all pounced on it at the same time, creating a writhing, snarling ball.

"I think I need to go to bed," mumbled Friedrich, his head resting on his crossed arms.

It had gotten cold. Janne ran her hands along her bare upper arms. Marlon stood up and went across the lawn until he disappeared into the darkness. Richard watched him go.

"To him it doesn't matter," I said, "whether it's day or night."

I stood up and got behind Janne. This time I didn't grab the handles, I put my hands on her shoulders. It seemed like an eternity ago that I had touched her, and even kissed her.

Janne put her head back. I leaned down and touched her forehead with my lips. In the dark her eyes were unfathomably deep, and she looked like a completely different girl, a stranger. She didn't protest as I kissed her first on the tip of her nose and then arrived at her lips. She tasted of the vinegar from the salad dressing and I ran the tip of my tongue along her lips.

Then I stood up straight again and saw that Richard was making a face like he had a toothache. I didn't know why I had to explain myself to Richard, so I leaned over Janne's backward-leaning head again. Her lips opened.

"It's a shame," she said.

"What's a shame?"

"That the camera's not running."

"Don't be such a camera whore." I kissed her again. But suddenly I felt bad for her, so tried to rephrase it more empathetically. "You probably couldn't pick anything up in this light anyway."

Marlon reappeared out of the darkness. I almost shouted because he appeared so quickly and silently. And from a completely different direction than he had gone off in.

Don't you touch her, I thought, and my fingers clenched

her shoulders so tightly that I probably caused her pain, but she didn't make a sound. *I* was here now.

Janne held her breath. Marlon turned away and went over to the cooling grill.

"Richard?" he called softly.

"Right here."

"Can I help with something? Cleaning up or something?"

Richard thought for a second. My hands moved from Janne's shoulders.

"Not much. There's a bit of trash on the lawn, can you grab that?"

"Sure," said Marlon.

"We could just as easily do it tomorrow."

"It doesn't matter."

"Exactly."

Marlon walked around the table slowly—I pulled Janne's wheelchair out of the way—stepped on a piece of tinfoil, picked it up, and tossed it onto the table. I could still see a plastic bag and a paper plate, but I didn't say anything. I suddenly felt guilty and refused to consider why.

Marlon turned abruptly and went slowly toward the villa, testing the ground with his toes before every step.

"What about them?" I pointed at the guru and Kevin.

"They can't stay out here. It's too cold at night," said Richard.

"But I'll bet they're heavy," I said.

Richard had found two wheeled cots in the shed. We hoisted first the guru and then Kevin onto the cots and pushed them into the shed. Then we grabbed two blankets from the house and Richard spread them over the two of them. The guru's face looked as if he was fighting with someone in his sleep. Sometimes his mouth formed mute words, his hands twitched and formed fists. Kevin lay there calm and smiling.

Tears still glimmered in the corners of his eyes. He looked like a girl.

"Little angel," said Janne as she sat there next to me, looking down at Kevin.

"Who? This queer?"

"Yeah."

Richard shook Friedrich's shoulder. Friedrich sat bolt upright, surprised, and then got up and wandered off toward the house. His amorphous body moved along behind Richard, slowly slogging along like a gigantic snail.

And Janne and I were alone.

She sat next to the grill and held her hands, shivering, over the coals. I pushed a few plates together on the table. I was oddly calm, and my hands weren't trembling.

"Janne," I mumbled. "Tell me, what can I do for you, Janne?"

She kept holding her hands closer and closer to the coals until they were practically touching them.

"Don't burn yourself."

"They're not hot anymore," she answered dully.

I went to her, squatted in front of her, and pulled her arm to me. I kissed her dirty hand and put it on my cheek. Her eyes were so dark that I barely recognized her.

"I love you."

"Bullshit." Janne tried to pull her hand away, but I didn't let her. "Stop," she said.

I took her other hand, blew the ashes off it, and put it to my lips.

"Don't be so bitter. Everybody loves you. You don't have to pretend."

"Like you have any clue." Suddenly she started crying.

I hadn't reckoned with this. I never thought she would ever cry in front of me. And that the tears would be so big and glitter in the moonlight as they rolled down Janne's cheeks.

"You look so beautiful when you cry," I said.

She pulled away from me and hit me in the face. With the palm of her hand, on the cheek, a weak awkward slap. It didn't even hurt. Still, it was the second smack of the day for my poor face. For a second I was shocked, then I approached the wheel-chair from the other side.

"Don't forget the other cheek," I said, smiling.

"You're an idiot. Do you not understand what you said?"

"You look so beautiful when you cry."

"Exactly."

Now she really started to sob. It was no longer single tears but torrents that left a wet trail on her face. She sniffled. It didn't look so nice anymore. Her eyes swelled and narrowed to slits. Her nose was probably all red, too, but you couldn't really tell in the dark. She sobbed like an old lady at a funeral and her shoulders trembled.

I put my arm around her. The tears tasted salty, what else.

"Don't cry," I said. "Look, you have no reason to cry. And you look most beautiful of all when you smile. Stop crying. You'll have your movie and your face will look down from all the billboards and smile, everyone will recognize you and you'll have to give autographs."

She shook her head. I pushed her over to the house and up the ramp. She gestured with her hand that she wanted to go straight to her room. Maybe she was afraid to be seen because she didn't look as good at that moment as she usually did. She kept turning her face away from me the whole time.

"You have to stop this bullshit," I said. "It's ridiculous."

"Then take off your glasses."

"You don't know what you're saying."

"Of course I do. Take them off, they're stupid."

"Screw you, Janne," I said.

She rolled into her room ahead of me; I followed her and sat down on the bed.

She rolled over to the dresser and pulled out a bright white shawl and put it around her shoulders, shivering. Then she rolled over to the mirror and grabbed her hairbrush. I watched her. Nothing could be more beautiful than watching a girl brush her hair. Of course it was even more beautiful if the girl was yours.

"Do you want to marry me, Janne?" I asked. "Right now, or when we're older—it doesn't matter to me."

She laughed. Watching the brush glide through her dense, shiny hair had a hypnotizing effect on me. I had to yawn so wide that my jaw cracked. I untied the laces of my sneakers, took them off, stretched out on the bed, and buried my nose in the pillows.

I was woken up by someone shining a flashlight in my face. I tried to push it away. But it wasn't a flashlight after all but a ray of sunlight, so I had to move away from it. My nose tickled and I ran a hand over it and noticed a strand of black hair between my fingers.

Suddenly it all came back to me and I sat up.

Janne was sleeping next to me. We were sharing a blanket. She was under it and I was on top of it. She was wearing a long nightgown with lace trim. On anyone else it would have looked absurd. Janne's hair was in a ponytail. The nightgown had slipped down over one shoulder.

It was light out, way too light out. At home I always kept the shades down. I went to straighten my sunglasses but my hand found nothing but air.

I didn't have to look for long. They were sitting on the dresser. Right next to the hairbrush.

Fucking hell, I thought.

I climbed carefully across Janne, who was breathing evenly, and walked on my tiptoes across the room and slid the glasses onto my nose. I turned around again. Janne looked unimaginably beautiful. I had spent the night in her bed and slept through it all.

It was a gorgeous morning. Friedrich, with suds up to his elbows, was scrubbing the grill grates out on the lawn. Kevin was still quietly snoring in the cot. The guru wasn't there.

"Did he take off?" I asked Friedrich, pointing at the empty stretcher.

"Showering." Friedrich wiped his face with his forearm, leaving soap foam on his eyebrows.

It looked like there had been an orgy on the lawn. Empty red wine bottles lying around under the table. Paper plates and bits of tinfoil fluttering in the wind. A little tabby cat sat on the table licking the salad bowl out.

I went back into the house and looked through the kitchen cabinets for a garbage bag. Couldn't find one so I grabbed a shopping bag instead. Ran into the guru, his face looked rumpled and he reeked of aftershave.

"Yes, I'm ashamed," he said. "I just can't understand how it happened."

I shrugged my shoulders. He might as well feel bad—it never hurt anyone.

"Is anyone else injured?"

I couldn't help laughing. Then I took the shopping bag outside and began to pick up the trash.

We planned to have breakfast in the garden together around noon. An hour beforehand I started knocking on Janne's door.

"Can't right now," she called, sounding happy, and I wondered how she knew it was me who was knocking. Or whether she thought it was somebody else. Or whether she even cared. Every time I thought about her taking off my glasses, I got chills down my spine.

Kevin was standing in our room complaining of a migraine, trying to get a pain reliever out of Marlon. Marlon said he didn't have any.

"That can't be true," Kevin whined, grabbing Marlon's T-shirt. "I can tell you have some. Look again."

I watched this play and weighed my desire to steer clear of Marlon against the need to talk to him. I felt like a pig, but a lucky pig.

So I decided to wait on my bed until Marlon had gotten rid of Kevin. Then at some point Kevin started to cry. I couldn't watch. I jumped up and starting rummaging around in my suitcase for my pills. I pushed one out of the blister pack and handed it to Kevin.

"It's good for everything," I said. "Consider yourself warned."

"You are my savior." Kevin pressed the hand with the pill to his forehead theatrically and put his other hand to his heart. The he blew a kiss to Marlon and, when he didn't react, another one to me, and then minced out of the room.

*

"Marlon," I said when we were finally alone. "I have to talk to you."

He was standing sideways to me with his hands in his pockets. He swayed back and forth. Somehow it reminded me of a tiger behind bars.

"Marlon," I said. "I really don't know how to say this. The problem is that you look absolutely perfect, even if you can't tell, and I am as ugly as the night and always will be. You can't possibly understand what that means. Not only that, you're cool, and I seem to have forever lost the ability to strike the right tone."

"Your phone rang all night," he interrupted.

My cell. I picked it up. I hadn't looked at it a single time since we got here. I had forgotten to send Claudia a message to say I'd arrived safely. She was probably worried sick. She might not have had the guru's number, either. She didn't even know exactly where we were.

I tipped over the chair as I searched for my phone in my suitcase, in the wardrobe, and finally found it in a jacket pocket. I had eleven missed calls, all from Claudia. She started dialing me yesterday night and didn't stop until the early morning hours. There was only one text, from a number I didn't recognize. I read it first. It said: "Marek our father is died come cwick. Ferdi."

At first I took it for a joke. Somebody was trying to trick me. Some huckster wanted me to call that fraudulent number and it would charge me hundreds of euros. If not for those five letters. Ferdi. Ferdi was the little son of my father and my former au pair. My half-brother who I'd never seen. The baby in that photo six years ago. Ferdinand. Claudia had sighed, "How could you do that to a child?"

Suddenly my knees buckled and I was afraid to listen to Claudia's messages. She hadn't sent me any texts because she wanted to tell me directly. I did not want to hear it directly. I wanted to hide my phone under a pillow, lock the door to the room, and go have breakfast. I didn't want anything to do with this.

Marlon came closer. No matter what everybody said, I no longer believed he was really blind. He asked, "What is it?" and I held out the phone with the text on it. He didn't move.

"I got a message." Then I read it to him.

"What's Ferdi?" asked Marlon.

I didn't answer.

"And is it your father who's dead?"

Again I said nothing.

"This brother, does he have a strange sense of humor?"

"He's still little," I said. "Six or so."

"Then you need to get going," said Marlon. "To the funeral."

I had no idea what was to be done. What I should do or say.

I felt like a first grader who'd accidentally wandered into an empty classroom. I wondered whether I really needed to go to my father's funeral since we'd been out of touch for a while. But my father had visited me in the hospital, so I guess I also had to go to his funeral.

Just to be sure, I asked Marlon his opinion.

"Don't be crazy," he said.

I read the text again. It still said the same thing. *Marek our father is died come cwick. Ferdi.* The letters were all still there.

"Who was trying to reach you all night?" asked Marlon.

"My mother."

"Call her back."

"I'm afraid."

"Do it. It'll just get worse otherwise."

I nodded and dialed Claudia's number. And as soon as I heard her voice on the line I knew there was no hope that it had all been a misunderstanding.

A little brother, how cute," said Kevin. "Do you have a photo?"

Richard looked at him and shook his head. The guru was holding his head in his hands and still didn't look good. I clenched my phone as if somebody else would die if I let go of it.

Claudia had cried on the phone. I had grown accustomed to her never crying anymore. I was ready to do anything to keep it that way. And now this.

I truly didn't understand why she was even crying. Why she sobbed "why now," as if today was so much worse than yesterday or the day after tomorrow. He had left her, and she'd been happy without him for a long time now. They hadn't been in touch, at least as far as I knew. She still had Dirk, I thought tolerantly.

"Ach, Marek," she said after I asked her about that. "You really don't understand anything."

I sat at the breakfast table and they all stared at me. All so sorrowful and sympathetic, what I really wanted to do was shout at them that they should look at me with normal faces again now.

"He left us when I was little!" I said to try to wipe that look off their faces. "He didn't even call me on my birthday anymore or send me anything. I don't give a shit, do you understand?" No idea why my voice cracked.

The funny thing was that I didn't look at Janne at all. I

looked at Marlon. As soon as I'd come to the table with my phone in hand my heart hadn't skipped its usual beat at the sight of her. A pretty girl in a wheelchair. *Marek our father is died.* Now she was looking at me with the same affected look as the rest of them. I was back on the other side of the glass.

I got up and went across the lawn to the edge of the woods. I tried to make a call from there but the reception was no good. I kept dialing the number that the text had come from, it beeped, and then there was absolute silence on the line. Then I realized I should try from a different spot. As soon as I walked to a spot with better reception, the phone rang. It was Claudia.

I was relieved that her voice was halfway recognizable this time.

"The funeral is in four days," said Claudia. "I'm afraid I won't be able to pick you up before that. I have to help Tamara, she's completely out of sorts. You'll have to take the train. Can you manage that? Or should I send Dirk to get you?"

"Do I really have to?" I asked.

"Marek, I'm begging you. I know it's difficult. I know you're . . . with your new friends. But these things happen when they happen. He is after all . . . your father."

"I haven't had a real father for ages," I said.

"If you only knew," said Claudia.

I sat on my suitcase beneath the information board that had no information at all. The train back to Berlin was supposed to come in half an hour. They all wanted to take me to the station but I refused. I had said that I wanted to be alone and that seemed to make sense to them. I also didn't want the farmer and his tractor. I pulled my suitcase the long way, staying on the paved path, and my thoughts rattled in rhythm with the wheels.

They gathered around me to say goodbye and I set off quickly and didn't look back even once. I had a lump in my throat but I couldn't tell if it was because of my father or Janne or general Rottweiler-weltschmerz. It felt as if I'd been here for weeks, not two nights, one of which was awful and the other would have been the most beautiful night of my life if I hadn't have slept through it. I tried to imagine myself going to another group meeting back in Berlin and I started laughing.

The loudspeaker crackled loudly and a few minutes later the regional train pulled in. I hoisted up my suitcase. The train was nearly empty and nobody looked at me. With my index finger I felt my face under my sunglasses to make sure nothing had changed over the last couple of days. Everything was the same as ever. If my father had seen me again it would have cost him a few nights of sleep for sure. At least in that regard he'd been lucky.

Claudia had sent me the address, with annotations, in a text. My father had lived in a village near Frankfurt called

Einhausen, the same place where he and I had both been born. After he had discovered his love for our au pair, Claudia had gone back to Berlin with me. My father was born and bred in the state of Hesse and had his office there where his family had lived for generations.

I had to switch trains in Berlin, Hannover, and Frankfurt. The ride seemed like it would never end. The phone stuck in my hand. Claudia kept sending texts, where was I and how was I feeling. I wasn't feeling a thing.

I didn't have a phone number for Janne. Not even the guru's number or anybody else's number. Maybe I had the list with everyone's contact info stuck in my suitcase somewhere, but probably not. Marlon would now have Janne to himself in Marenitz—oddly enough that thought didn't upset me at all.

What was funny was that I almost missed Marlon more.

An old lady in a blue uniform, with swollen feet, pushed the refreshment cart down the aisle. Badly damaged venous valves, I thought, and I ordered myself a coffee. She took my coins without counting them and handed me a lukewarm paper cup.

People were not in such sound condition as I'd always thought. I let my gaze sweep over the backs of heads that I could see from my seat. Some of these people probably thought they were healthy and always would be. I used to think the same thing. My father, too, probably, and now he was dead.

Claudia had said that I should take a taxi from the station. They didn't have time to pick me up because they needed to stay with Tamara and the little one. It was tougher than I thought to get a taxi. There wasn't a single one waiting at the tiny station. I walked all around it, startling a couple of teenagers with beers in their hands. I wondered whether I'd be standing here if my father had used a condom with our au pair. Then with a sigh I opened the map function on my phone and tried to figure out which way I had to walk.

As I set out across a parking lot a taxi showed up. A man with a black mustache sat at the wheel, probably a Turk rather than a Pakistani I decided as I slid into the back seat next to some bags. I told him the address. He looked at me in the rearview mirror.

"Who did that?" he asked.

"A Rottweiler." It had been a while since anyone had asked about it. About a week. An eternity.

"My brother-in-law had a Rottweiler." The Turk sounded as if he was doing me a favor telling me. "Real nice. But such teeth!"

"If it was up to me I'd have them all ground into bonemeal. As far as I'm concerned, that could go for every dog on the planet."

The Turk shook his head. "Not all. My brother-in-law's Rottweiler is nice. But you really look different. What does your girl say?"

"She's getting off with a blind guy," I summed up our complicated love triangle for him.

"The girl blind, too?"

If only it were that easy, I thought. "She's in a wheelchair and is the prettiest girl in the world."

"Shit," said the Turk understandingly.

After ten minutes I realized he was fucking with me. Einhausen wasn't that big. It was a dump with ten thousand residents, you could *walk* all the way through town in fifteen minutes.

"We almost there?"

"Almost there," the Turk echoed. "What are you here for?"

"My father died," I said and couldn't believe that he was suddenly pissed off and yelled that I shouldn't fuck with him. It took a lot of effort to convince him to still take me all the way to my destination.

I stood before a gray box that was mostly hidden behind a meter-high hedgerow that smelled like cough syrup. On the gate was a plaque with my last name on it, engraved in rounded letters. The place was a nightmare in concrete. After all those years in our historic landmarked building, I wasn't prepared for this. For a second I wondered if maybe what came between my parents wasn't Tamara at all but rather aesthetic differences. Those were harder to overcome than a pregnant au pair. Even under happier circumstances I wouldn't have been happy to enter this mausoleum. But the taxi was already gone and the driver had kept my change. I rang the bell.

It buzzed and I pushed open the gate. The yard was wide and lined with low hedges that also reminded me of a cemetery. I headed toward the door, from which hung a wreath, that also reminded me of a . . . The door opened.

I attempted a smile so painstaking that it pulled at my ear.

In the doorway appeared a tyke with spiky blond hair, just like mine had been. He was wearing Star Wars pajamas and slippers with bunny ears. His expression suddenly became the famous painting by Edvard Munch. Then he disappeared in a flash and his Scream echoed from somewhere inside the house. As I got nearer to the door I could hear him swearing loudly that he would never do *it* again if the man with the hat would just please, please go away.

And then I landed in Tamara's arms.

Unlike the old days I didn't have to stand on my tiptoes to be able to look down Tamara's shirt. I flushed thinking how present Tamara's breasts had been during that year at our place. As far as I could tell, my perspective was the only thing that had changed in the equation.

"Sincere condolences," I mumbled, blindsided by the slew of postpubescent thoughts hitting me. Then I finally looked her in the eyes.

In the past I'd always found Tamara very pretty. That was basically still true, even though my standard of beauty had shifted significantly because of Janne. Compared to Janne, any other woman looked like a rough draft And at the moment Tamara wasn't exactly bursting with life. She had red splotches on her cheeks and dark rings under her bloodshot eyes. She looked about as old as Claudia. And just to prove it, Claudia came up beside her.

"My sweetie," said Claudia, her lips trembling as she stretched out her arms to me.

I didn't understand whatever it was she whispered in my ear. She probably passed on her condolences, too. I said, "Likewise," and looked at her so as not to have to look at Tamara or at the decor inside this concrete grotto. The stone floor beneath my feet was black with white specks, and somewhere farther back a fireplace with a curved mantel crept into my field of vision.

But I couldn't count the lines on my mother's face forever, so I turned back to Tamara with a sigh. Everything that had happened to me leading up to this moment suddenly rushed through my head and I wanted to turn away to spare the young widow's nerves.

But Tamara walked around me so she was standing directly in front of me. She grabbed my chin with her hand. Spellbound, she scanned my face, but when she went to remove my sunglasses I shoved her hand aside. I broke out in a sweat. I saved myself by staring once again at her cleavage.

"You look . . . " Tamara exhaled. My cheeks began to tingle. Claudia coughed quietly.

"Tammy," she said, "I think you need to check on the little one."

I sat on the leather sofa next to Claudia, who was looking through some folder as if her life depended on it. On the floor above us, war had broken out. Tamara screamed in a language I took for Ukrainian, and Ferdi answered in German.

"I AM NOT GOING DOWNSTAIRS!!"

Ukrainian chatter.

"I'M SCARED ANYWAY!"

Ukrainian chatter.

"I DON'T BELIEVE YOU! PAPA NEEDS TO COME HOME!!"

Claudia looked at the ceiling and wiped a tear from her cheek.

"Leave the boy alone," I shouted. "He's not the only person who's afraid of me."

Tamara's Ukrainian rose to a pitch that rattled my bones.

"HE IS NOT AND NEVER WAS MY BROTHER!" the child screamed.

"Marek, come upstairs so you can meet each other," shouted Tamara.

"NOOOOOOO!! PLEASE NO!! PLEASE NO!!!"

There was nothing else I could do, so I covered my ears with my hands. My nerves weren't so strong at the moment either. Claudia played as if she was just continuing to read something in her folder. Though it had been a long time since she flipped the page. I wondered whether it was her heartbeat or mine that I was hearing. I took one hand off my ear and took another apple from the glass bowl. I'd already eaten four just out of nervousness. There were three left. The hard chewing was calming.

Tamara came running down the stairs and made another attempt at hugging me.

"I'm sorry, Marek. Ferdi is stubborn. You were the same way once, heaven knows. I apologize. It'll get better."

"Hmmmhmmm." My mouth was stuffed.

"The boy has just lost his father," Claudia said almost as an aside.

"Which one?"

"Both." Claudia looked at Tamara over her glasses. "Presumably both boys."

Two hours later I was pining for the villa in Marenitz. It was unbearable. I had no idea what I was supposed to do here. Claudia made it easy on herself by keeping her nose buried in the paperwork and pulling something out every once in a while for Tamara.

"You need to copy this. This needs to be filed. This is for the life insurance."

"Okay," answered Tamara without looking at the documents.

Ferdi refused to come downstairs as long as I was in the living room. He shouted something about frightening glasses. Claudia assured Tamara not very convincingly that it wasn't so bad. I said I was used to children crossing the street because of me. Adults, too. Tamara looked at me. "Why?"

I wasn't sure whether she was pretending or she was really that stupid. I couldn't remember anymore what she'd been like in the brains department. I watched as she fumed around her tiled home, changed outfits, called somebody, broke down crying, screamed at Ferdi, made tea and left it sitting around, went out to the postbox to get the latest condolence cards. The entire town of Einhausen seemed in a hurry to proclaim their sorrow over Father in writing. In some envelopes was money that made its way into Tamara's jeans.

"You should write it all down," said Claudia. "You need to keep track so you can send personal thank you notes to everyone."

"I will." Tamara tossed the envelopes behind the sofa.

I had to admit that my father had chosen a death that you didn't need to be ashamed of. He didn't die miserably of cancer or just keel over, leaving me to worry about what health problems he'd passed on to me. He died while climbing a mountain in Switzerland.

"He climbed mountains?" I asked, pleasantly surprised. The father I remembered had a big belly and hamster cheeks, and everything on him drooped. The idea of him outfitted for a climb, on the side of a mountain, exceeded my powers of imagination.

"He had just started." Tamara didn't bother to try to wipe away the steady stream of tears. "And now he's fallen!" She buried her face in a sofa cushion.

I patted her back awkwardly. "At least it was a cool way to die."

"It's an idiotic way to die," groaned Tamara through the pillow. "Why does someone who's nearly sixty suddenly need to start climbing mountains?"

"What do you mean nearly sixty? He was only two years older than me." Claudia looked up from her folder for a moment.

Tamara gave her a look that said to her it didn't make much of a difference.

Ferdi sat under the table. He'd been hiding under there since I'd left the guest room and come downstairs. The table-cloth hung down and sometimes rippled. Now and then I saw the flash of a dark eye.

"Ferdi, *durak, perestan*," said Tamara.

"Not in front of the child," Claudia said.

Tamara reached out her arm and pushed my hair to the side.

"Your sunglasses make a monster out of you," she said without acknowledging Claudia's comment. "Otherwise you're totally sweet. You always were. I would like to have adopted you. I thought it was awful that you left here straight away."

I looked over at Claudia. She continued to study the folder. Her chin looked a little more square than usual.

There wasn't another moment of peace.

The village mortician came, a man who looked like he had just stepped out of a Viagra commercial, with silver hair and a tailored suit, his face so serious it made you sick. He shook my hand and said he couldn't find adequate words to express his feelings about my loss. I nodded.

He also had a thick folder under his arm and exchanged it for the even thicker one Claudia had prepared for him. The three of them sat at the table and talked, that is, Claudia and the mortician talked and Tamara sniffled into her handkerchief. They had invited me to join their roundtable but I declined. I had nothing to say anyway, and I had no desire to sniffle.

I sat with a photo album in my lap but couldn't bring myself to open it. Tamara had insisted that I look at it. Claudia agreed that it could be helpful. Oddly enough, she herself had no desire to sit with me while I did. The album began shortly before Ferdi's birth and took in his first year. Five more albums waited in a stack on the coffee table.

I didn't want to snub Tamara, and anyway I was a little curious. But I wasn't prepared for the naked photo of the two of them, Tamara heavily pregnant, my father presumably not. I covered his nakedness with my thumb and peered over at Claudia. I had no idea that my father had been so frisky. There certainly weren't any photos like that in *my* baby album.

I flipped quickly past the first shots of the slop-covered, purple thing, too.

"You can compare them to your baby pictures," Tamara had suggested as she'd dug out the albums.

"He doesn't have any anymore," said Claudia insensitively.

"What? Where did they go?"

"He destroyed them all. Last year."

"Really? Why?" Tamara turned to me. I acted as if I hadn't heard her. I was pissed off at Claudia.

I leafed through the heavy pages. Ferdi in a stroller, Ferdi in a high chair, Ferdi in a baby carrier. Where was my father? Here, at the beach. He was building a sand castle, and Ferdi was crawling away from it. He had built sand castles with me, too. And he probably wasn't in the other photos because he had taken them all.

"What was he like?" I asked Tamara.

She waved her hand. "You know yourself."

Only I didn't know anymore. When my parents were still together, Claudia usually stayed with me, and she'd always been in a bad mood. My father had worked day and night but despite that he was always in a good mood as far as I could remember. He had loved his work. I liked to hear his stories while we cooked Sunday dinner, stories about murders without bodies, crooked witnesses who were too stupid to keep their stories straight, and judges he'd made livid by making sixty accusations of judicial bias per session. I kind of worshipped him for having such an exciting job. Not like Claudia, who just helped wives negotiate more money out of their divorces and never talked about her clients on principle.

Suddenly the memories overwhelmed me and took my breath away. I hadn't known that they were all still there. How my father and I would go shopping in Einhausen on Saturday if for a change he didn't have to disappear to his office. He carefully picked out stalks of rhubarb and talked with people at the weekly market. Everyone knew him. He asked the sellers about their families, they told him about their daughters-in-law and grandchildren. He was constantly greeted, people called him "Herr Barrister"; it didn't bother him that he constantly had to stop and shake hands, on the contrary. They knew his parents and grandparents and in the unofficial rankings he was somewhere between the mayor and the parish minister and he basked in the recognition. I walked along holding his hand, looking at the shoes of the people who interrupted us while we were shopping, and I was unaware how much rubbed off on me. The only one who seemed troubled by the majestic appearance of Herr Barrister and his crown prince was Claudia. She also missed Berlin and called Einhausen "Swinehausen."

And for the first time I realized that everything could have been totally different than I'd always believed. Maybe my father took up with Tamara only after Claudia decided she wanted to split up with him. What did I know. I had never asked her and didn't think this was exactly the right moment either. No idea if there would ever be a better moment.

At dinner, Ferdi sat with us at the table for the first time. Tamara had probably bribed him. His blond hair was standing up like the wet feathers of a newly hatched chick, and his eyes were glued to the contents of his plate. It didn't seem like the right time to discuss the correct usages of died and dead with him. Tamara had cooked cream of wheat for everyone, a quick meal, and, as she explained to Claudia, in her homeland, "oddly enough, a mourning dish."

Ferdi sprinkled sugar and cinnamon over his bowl by the spoonful. A puff of powder went up as he began to stir it in.

"Ferdi, *perestan*," said Tamara. *Perestan* was apparently something like a second name for him.

"Ferdi, have you shown your cool older brother with the unbelievably nice sunglasses your toy cars?"

Ferdi shook his head and shoved an empty spoon into his mouth.

"Marek would really like to see them. Isn't that right, Marek, you want to see Ferdi's toy cars?"

"Oh yes." I straightened my glasses. "That's why I came here, actually."

Ferdi risked a quick glance at me. There was a bottomless horror in his eyes.

"I have plenty of my own at home," I quickly added. "But will you show me yours?"

He shook his head quickly and adamantly.

"*Fu, nekrasivo*, Ferdi."

"Leave him alone," said Claudia flatly.

"Why do you look like that?" Ferdi suddenly asked, shoving a full spoon into his mouth this time, chewing the bite busily, and looking around as if he hadn't said anything.

"It was a Rottweiler," I said with the usual melancholy. And when he looked up uncomprehendingly, "A Rottweiler is a big, mean dog with really sharp teeth."

"See, Ferdi," said Tamara. "Do you still want a dog?"

He nodded just as quickly and decisively as he had shaken his head just before.

"Papa promised me a dog," he said, slumping closer to the table. And then I saw that he was crying.

Maybe I had never really seen a child crying before. Maybe I had never really understood why on earth they would be crying. But now, as I looked at Ferdi's little wet, contorted face, I suddenly had a lump in my throat. I was ready to do anything to get him to stop crying. I didn't want him ever to cry again.

"Ferdi," I said. "Stop crying. I hate dogs more than anything else in the world, but I'll get you one."

Claudia put down her spoon and looked at me.

"Actually I need two dogs," I mused aloud. "I recently promised a girl a dog as well."

Ferdi stopped chewing. For the first time, his dark eyes rested on my face for a bit of time. Probably all he saw was his future dog because suddenly he started smiling. I had never seen him smile before. I was amazed that he even could. I stared at him with my mouth open until Tamara tried to pinch my thigh under the table and missed the mark.

That evening Ferdi, at Tamara's prompting, loudly said "goodnight"—first to Claudia and then also to me. He looked at his toes in his red no-slip socks as he did.

"Sleep well, my dear," Claudia answered sweetly. I looked at her. She had never spoken to me in such an artificially sweet tone.

"Sleep well, gnome," I said.

Tamara blew us both kisses.

"She likes being the center of attention, don't you think?" asked Claudia after Tamara had disappeared upstairs with Ferdi riding her piggyback.

"She's still a child herself," said Claudia.

"She's at least twenty-four years old."

"Exactly."

Claudia sat on the leather sofa, snuggled a throw pillow, and looked somehow lost. Upstairs Tamara began to sing. A few minutes later Ferdi joined in. Claudia looked up at the ceiling and stealthily wiped her face.

Maybe she was thinking about how nice it was when I was Ferdi's age, sweet, blond, and with a real face.

"Is he really gone? Forever?" I asked.

"No idea," said Claudia. "I can't get rid of the feeling that this is all a farce. I just can't believe it. I keep thinking the door is going to open any minute and he'll walk in." She covered her face with her hands.

I had to think about how one day in the hospital, after the pain had subsided, I looked in the mirror and imagined that everything was the same way it had always been.

I had the guest room in the attic, with angled walls and a skylight window through which you could definitely have seen the stars on a cloudless night. The house was gigantic, Claudia was on a floor below that I hadn't even seen yet. Ferdi's room must have been there, too, and Tamara's, which she had until a few days ago shared with my father. There was also a sauna, a huge wine cellar, and a fitness room full of machines.

"Was it like this for us before, too?" I had asked Claudia, but she hadn't realized I meant it approvingly. "Not quite this bad," she had said. "I can show you our old house at some point if you'd like."

I gratefully declined.

I put on my jeans and opened the bedroom door. A note was stuck to the outside of the door. "*Maritschek, we have a lot of things to take care of. Help yourself to breakfast. Kisses, T.*" I ripped off the note and stuck it in my pocket.

I walked down the stairs to the next floor. The bathroom door was open, I looked in, and I saw a colorful little toilet seat and a plastic stool in front of the sink, which was smeared with toothpaste. There were bras hanging everywhere with cats and mice and roses on them. I picked one up and let it dangle from my pointer finger, averting my eyes as usual from the bathroom mirror. I couldn't help thinking of my father and how such a momentous wife-swap really could give you a heart attack.

On the door next to the bathroom were dancing wooden

letters that spelled out FERDINAD. The second N must have been dancing at another party somewhere. I opened the door and peeked in. I tried to ignore the sting I felt as I looked at the dark wooden pirate ship bed with a giant captain's wheel on it. There was a big Ikea rug with street markings on it that reminded me of one I'd had in my room not so long ago. On it a multi-car pileup had been staged. Flying Lego debris probably symbolized a natural disaster.

I pushed the cars aside with my foot and sat down in the middle of the rug. I picked up a little convertible and drove it along one of the streets printed on the rug. Then I began to put together the Lego pieces. The ones within my immediate reach weren't always what I wanted. I looked around the room for the right pieces until I found a big container of Legos.

When I was finished I had built a parking garage with a fence around it and had parked all the cars inside. In front of the garage I built an avenue lined with trees and flowerbeds. When I was done I looked up at the ceiling, which was covered with a mixed-up array of clouds and stars, and then I let my eyes drop to the documents and photos the walls were papered with.

I stood up, brushed some construction materials off my pants, and went closer. Ferdi had received a commendation from the tooth fairy for good brushing and a certificate for finishing third in a ski race at a Swiss ski school. In a photo nearby he was holding up the medal he'd won and looked as if he felt personally insulted. In the photo to the right of that he was smiling in Tamara's arms, and when my eyes lit on the next photo my heart stood still. At first I thought it was another shot of Ferdi, only looking weirdly a bit older and taller than now. And then I realized it was me.

I flew out of Ferdi's room and closed the door a little harder than necessary. Down in the kitchen I opened the refrigerator with trembling hands. I examined rows of pickle jars, moldy cheese rinds, and cold cuts that had gone green. I tried to count how many days my father had been dead and how long he must have been traveling before that. I didn't come to any conclusive number. I sniffed the open milk suspiciously and looked for a while for the expiration date on the egg carton.

On the stove was a pot with the dried out oatmeal leftovers. I put it in the sink, grabbed another pan from a hook on the wall, and just to be safe, washed it.

The coffee machine was as big as a spaceship and about as easy to operate. I pushed a few buttons and several things lit up red and steam came out the side. Before it could explode I pulled out the plug and opted for instant cappuccino powder and a couple slices of toast from a loaf of bread I spotted up in a cabinet.

I had just put the fork with fried egg to my mouth when the doorbell rang. I gulped down the bite of egg and hurried upstairs since my sunglasses were still sitting somewhere in my room in the attic. As I looked for them, put them on, took them off so I could pull on a T-shirt, and then ran back downstairs, it rang a few more times. I threw open the door.

On the front step was a solid woman with a strikingly small head, or maybe just a too-short haircut. I could tell she was a pro by the fact that she didn't flinch at the sight of me. The only people who were so firm and persistent were those who had their eyes on a specific goal. I was about to learn hers. She was the headmistress of Ferdi's school, Frau Meyerling.

Somewhat surprised, I stepped slightly to the side. Ferdi was out with his mother, I said, and wanted to close the door again and get back to my eggs, but she pushed me gently but determinedly out of the way and was suddenly standing in the house. There was nothing else I could do but close the door even though she was now on the wrong side of it. Then I repeated that neither Ferdi nor his mother were home in case she was a bit hard of hearing.

"No problem, I have time." To my horror, she slipped her patent leather shoes off her feet and looked at me as if sizing me up. "Who are you?"

"The brother," I mumbled.

"What brother?" She seesawed back and forth on her feet uncomfortably.

I explained—the look on her face said she was perplexed.

"A Rottweiler," I said before she asked.

"Did you wind him up?"

"I bit him first," I said.

"You'll ruin your eyes wearing sunglasses indoors."

"My mother says the same thing."

"Listen to your mother." She pulled a pack of cigarettes out of her bag, turned them wistfully in her hand, and then tossed them back into the bag.

"It's a no-smoking household, is it?" she asked in a kind of demanding tone. She probably thought that if I could wear sunglasses inside this was the type of place where anything was permitted.

"There's a small child living here," I said with as much disdain as if I worked for the national cancer society.

"I know, I know," she answered, sounding irritated. "Why do you think I'm here. I'm nervous."

I was nervous, too. I was also hungry, and my eggs were going to be as cold as the pseudo-cappuccino. But eating while this woman was sitting on the leather couch watching me was beyond my powers. Disappearing upstairs with the plate seemed impolite, and I had even less desire to offer her some of my painstakingly composed breakfast.

"Can I help you?" I finally asked. "I really have no idea how long they will be."

"It always takes a long time," she said. "Cases of death are time-consuming, you don't have to tell me. But I still need to speak to your mother."

What about, I wondered. She read the question on my face.

"It's about the little one."

"Did he get up to something?"

"Get up to something? No. He's an unobtrusive child. Supposedly he can write already, but I don't believe it. Boys pick it up more slowly. I need to tell your sister about the grief work we've arranged at the school. A death like this doesn't affect only the relatives."

"Hmm," I said.

"We're unsettled." She pulled out a folded and ironed handkerchief and held it up to the bags under her eyes. "I can still picture your brother-in-law . . . "

I interrupted her to explain once again how we were all related to each other. Maybe Tamara had the same sunglasses and the woman took us for blood relations on that basis.

"But these days there's a lot you can do to help a family absorb such a shock." She tucked away her handkerchief again and her businesslike demeanor returned. "Our entire team wishes to support your sister during this difficult time. She should know that she is not alone, and neither is Frederic."

"Ferdinand."

"Just as I said. Can I assume that material concerns are not a worry?" She looked at me with an attentiveness I didn't like.

"No idea," I said. "Maybe my father left nothing but debts behind."

"Your father?" she asked. "Is he dead as well?"

I opened my mouth but the key jangled in the lock right at that moment.

"I picked out a nice big urn," called Ferdi.

We could have all been in something approaching a good mood except that Frau Meyerling seemed to work against it at every opportunity. She put on a mournful face. Then she walked with her hand extended toward Tamara, who wasn't expecting to find a visitor at home and didn't even know who she was. Tamara met the handshake with her jaw hanging open. In her other hand she was holding her left shoe, which she had already slipped off. The tall heel pointed aggressively in Frau Meyerling's direction.

Frau Meyerling took this as the perfect moment to break

into tears. I thanked my stars that she hadn't put so much effort into her performance for me. Now with a groan she squatted down in front of Ferdi. He took a few steps back, shocked.

"Can I hug you, Frederic?"

"No," said Ferdi, and his eyes, too, filled with tears.

"We're all sad." Frau Meyerling sniffled as proof. "The entire kindergarten is crying with you, Fred. I really liked your father."

I leaned against the doorframe and put my hands in my pockets so as not to use them to grab Frau Meyerling around the throat.

"Don't be ashamed if you need to cry." She stood up slowly. As she did, she braced herself on Ferdi's little shoulder, nearly causing him to buckle. Now she had him really wound up and he started sobbing loudly; my fists itched to be used. If I were a Rottweiler, I would have been in desperate need of a muzzle.

"Leave him alone," I said. "Cry with adults if you feel like you need to."

"Young man." She turned to me and pushed her glasses further up the bridge of her nose. "I have given seminars about helping children deal with grief. Do you really wish to tell me how to act?"

She was still holding Ferdi by the shoulder. My throat caught as I tried to come up with an answer. Claudia got there first.

"Would you like a cup of coffee?" She nudged Tamara, who immediately got to work. "Please sit down. I'm the ex-wife of the deceased, and the young man with the fashionable sunglasses is my son Marek, and I thank you for taking the time to pay us a visit."

Frau Meyerling had to let go of Ferdi to shake Claudia's hand, and that was probably Claudia's intent. Ferdi scurried off like a shot as Tamara pushed on the buttons of her space-ship. I wanted to follow Ferdi but he had already disappeared into his room and slammed the door shut. Then it sounded as if a bunch of matchbox cars were being thrown against the wall. Feeling like a coward I went up the stairs to my room on the floor above and didn't go back downstairs until the door had been locked behind Frau Meyerling.

Her sweet perfume still hung in the air, and there were pamphlets with candles and angels scattered all over the place. I picked one up, it was about a grief support group for children. I gathered them up and stacked them neatly, and turned around to go look for a wastepaper basket.

"Everyone deals with things their own way," said Claudia quietly.

"She's a vulture," I said. "She doesn't really give a shit."

Claudia shook her head and tossed a thick catalogue onto the coffee table. I looked at it for a second, it was an urn catalogue. Ferdi had already taken care of picking one out. Tamara was rattling things around over in the refrigerator. She was pulling out all the moldy stuff and stacking it up on the windowsill.

"By the way, we have a problem." Claudia was flipping through the catalogue again, urns made of mahogany and marble.

"Really?"

"Yes. The Swiss authorities now say they can't release the body until somebody has identified it."

"Is it possible that they made a mistake?" asked Tamara.

My heart leapt. That's exactly what I had been thinking the whole time.

"Impossible. It's just a formality. But there's still no way around it."

"And that just occurred to them now?!" Tamara yelled shrilly. "The funeral is already scheduled."

A jar of pickles fell from her hand and shattered on the tiles. The brine splattered in every direction. Tamara slid down the wall and slumped to the floor, covering her face with her hands.

The smashing glass had done something to me. I was unable to settle back down. Tamara's shoulders trembled, her sobs reached me on a time-delay, like thunder after the lightning. Claudia pushed me out of the way and squatted down next to her, put her arm around Tamara's shoulders, and rocked back and forth with her. Then something exploded over my head. Up in his room Ferdi had thrown my entire carefully constructed Lego parking garage against the wall.

"I can do it," I said.

Tamara said she wasn't up to it, and couldn't leave Ferdi alone anyway. Claudia dialed the phone with a stone face and turned away from Tamara, who continued to talk to her the whole time. The Swiss police were hard to reach, in trying to find the responsible party she was transferred ten different times only to end up back at the first person who'd answered. A body apparently couldn't be legally identified using photographs or a description; the only exception was if the dead party's dentist could certify the identity of the corpse by dental records.

"Is it really so complicated?" I asked. "I mean, who else could the body be? Can't they just use identifiable scars . . . ?"

"In-person identification or dental records," hissed Claudia with the phone wedged between her shoulder and ear as music tinkled from the earpiece. "There's no point in arguing over the logic, Marek, it's the law. Stop annoying me with stupid questions. Dental records would work, but it takes two weeks."

"That won't work." Tamara shook her head. "I can't take it for another two weeks."

"What can't you take? He'll be dead a good bit longer than two weeks," I said.

Claudia tried to stop me from speaking and nearly knocked my glasses off my face. Tamara stared blankly at a spot on the opposite wall. "One of us can go there with the funeral director when he goes to pick him . . . or, the body . . . up."

The soles of my feet stuck to the tile. They hadn't wiped up the pickle brine and there were pieces of broken glass all over the place. I found a bucket under the sink and gathered up the shards.

"I can do it," I said. "I'll go with the funeral director. I can identify him."

I hoped so anyway. We hadn't seen each other in a long time, but the Swiss police didn't need to know that. I'd get a recent photo from Tamara beforehand.

"You're still a child," said Tamara with a tear-streaked face. It seemed to me that if anyone here looked like a child—and was acting like one—it was her.

Nobody could tell my age now anyway, I said. That was never going to change.

"You'll have to show identification there," said Claudia wearily. But she didn't immediately reject the idea. On the contrary, she thought about my suggestion and something like hope flickered across her face. We'd all had a feeling who the job would fall to—fourteen hours in the car, half of them in the company of a corpse.

I fished a pickle out from under the kitchen cabinet, rinsed it off in the sink, and stuck it in my mouth.

And thought about Janne for the first time since I'd arrived.

C laudia was to be picked up at six in the morning by the funeral director to drive to Switzerland.

"You have to help Tamara, okay?" she said, pinching my cheek. In her other hand she had a cup of coffee that she kept perilously tilting. "While I'm gone you are the man of the house."

"And who am I when you are here?" I thought of Dirk again, Claudia hadn't said a word about him in the last two days and I wondered whether I needed to be worried. She looked tired and spent, her short hair standing up, dark rings beneath her eyes, only her lipstick was still its usual garish color and her skirt as short as ever. I kissed her on the cheek and saw the red veins shimmering through the skin.

"Take care of yourself," I said.

"Take care of her," she said. "And of the little one."

"Let's not go overboard," I said. "She stole your husband."

"What's she got for it now?" She pulled on my undamaged earlobe.

I stood and watched the long dark car pull up to the door. She waved before she climbed in.

I could have gone back to sleep for a few more hours, but instead I went to the coffee-spaceship and pushed on a couple of buttons. The indicator lights came on and once again it started to steam, but this time it didn't stop me. I pulled out the round filter like I'd seen Tamara do the day before and emptied it out over the trashcan. I found the bag of beans and poured some into the coffee mill. I hadn't expected the mill to be quite so loud. A noise like that would have made any normal person jump out of bed, but everything remained silent upstairs.

I no longer wondered why Claudia seemed in such a hurry to get down here once she'd heard the news of the death. Without her nothing happened in Swinehausen. Now, with her traveling for an entire day, I could see in my mind the way everything was immediately falling apart. How Ferdi would cry, hungry, unkempt, and totally neglected, how Tamara wouldn't even think she had to get out of bed, how the folder of important documents would end up in the wastepaper basket and the house would collapse and bury us all beneath marble slabs. I was the man of the house, that's what Claudia said to me, and that didn't sound like fun.

I sat down on a kitchen chair after I'd gotten rid of some more brochures about grief support groups. Somehow I didn't think Ferdi needed that sort of thing. I myself had rejected all kinds of offers for therapy in my time. Claudia had tried to bribe me with a home video system and a trip to America if only I'd been willing to dump my psychological junk onto a specialist, but I remained as steadfast as a stake. Until I'd landed in the arms of the guru, taken in by the most idiotic of lies: that I would see my life with completely different eyes in a week's time.

I took a similarly dim view of grief puppets and of painting nightmare images and of group arts and crafts projects. I was very conservative about such things. And I'd promised Ferdi a puppy even though I hated dogs.

I drank my espresso, which was passable, and thought again about Janne. The feeling of having forgotten her was baffling. Now she was here again, all I had to do was close my eyes in order to see her on the inside of my eyelids in her long dress, with a look on her face that said she'd like to bite my ear, too, and giving off a subtle smell of lime that was so fresh and so good and so bad at the same time that it suited her.

I knocked back the espresso, spat some coffee grounds that had strayed into my mouth into the sink, and went upstairs on tiptoes. Suddenly I just knew she had sent me a text message, maybe right at that moment, maybe during the night. Maybe she'd sat up the entire night, unable to sleep because she was so worried about me, waiting for an answer. I felt guilty and swore to myself never to let either Janne or my phone out of my sight again.

I couldn't find it at first, kept looking in various bags, under pillows and under the bed, until it fell out of a sock. I turned it on and waited for the list of missed calls and unread messages to appear, I waited for several minutes, it took a while to connect to the network. At some point it became clear that it wasn't necessary to wait any longer, because nobody had called and nobody had sent a message.

Marek, my bunny?" called Tamara as I went back downstairs with heavy steps to further my knowledge of the coffee machine. I wanted to drink three, maybe five cups, until my heart burst out of my ribs, nothing mattered to me now. I wanted to forget that I was the man of the house. I no longer consented to it. I hadn't seen Ferdi for the first six years of his life, and there was no fundamental reason I had to see him now. I didn't feel like answering Tamara, but she called out to me again.

"Has Claudia already left?" she asked as I entered her bedroom through the open door. She had sounded as if she was still half asleep, and that's just how it was. The bed was huge and the sheets striped; above the bed was a mirror and on the opposite wall a so-called erotic calendar. In another situation I might have risked a second glance at it. Next to Tamara was something big and poofy. It turned out to be a mangy man-sized teddy bear.

"Your best friend?" I asked, leaning against the doorframe, looking at Tamara and choking back a sort of hoarseness in my throat. I couldn't block out of my mind the question of whether she was naked under the covers. Both arms and both legs peeked out, a pile of clothes sat on the floor, the wardrobe door was open, and a Hello Kitty tank top dangled from a hanger hooked to the lamp.

"I can't fall asleep otherwise," said Tamara dully. "Without him, you understand."

"I understand." I couldn't take my eyes off her, the way she was stretched out and lounging, tussled hair in her face. She didn't look like a widow.

She stretched out her arm. Maybe just for the hell of it, but maybe to motion me closer. I went closer and sat down on the edge of the bed. Now I could smell her, a little sweat and perfume and a lot of woman, and for a second I felt dizzy. Maybe that's why I fell back onto the bed.

She'd thrown her arms around me and pulled me tightly to her. I gasped for air, a sound escaped from me that startled even me. Tamara let go of me suddenly. I protested against the acute sense of loneliness that arose as a result. Her bare feet tromped past me and into the bathroom, the water ran, I heard her gargle and spit, something hissed, and when she came back she didn't smell like a woman anymore but like a drugstore. No idea who kissed who first, but our mouths locked onto each other so fiercely, as if we could do something about each other's pain. I heard the teddy bear snarl and thought for a second it might be a real animal. I only became aware of myself again when Tamara held my mouth shut.

"Not so loud. The kid."

I lay next to her on my back and gasped for air, pressing the flat of my hand against my throat because I suddenly could no longer breathe. I tried to sit up, panicking. Tamara helped me to sit up and braced me from behind.

"Just keep breathing," she said, and it sounded a lot less friendly than anything else I'd heard from her in the last few days. "You're not dying, you're just . . . "

"Be quiet," I interrupted with my first lungful of air. The last thing I had in mind was discussing it with her. I lay back down and closed my eyes. Tamara smelled different again now, simultaneously like woman and man. She smelled of me.

Since I didn't know whether I should thank her or apologize, I just lay there. I stayed until I heard her get up and go into the bathroom. When I heard the water running I felt like getting up and running, too.

When I woke up the house was as silent as during the night. The clock radio next to the bed said it was four in the afternoon. I jumped out of bed, looked down at myself, and remembered everything. I grabbed a puke-yellow towel from the doorknob and wrapped it around myself. Then I called for Tamara and Ferdi but nobody answered.

I went down the stairs and slumped onto the couch in the living room. I'd really outdone myself: Claudia had barely left and I'd already molested my father's widow and slept away the rest of the day. If something awful happened to them now, like if they were run over by a truck because Tamara was even more distracted than before as a result of our adventure, then it would all be my fault. I may have been deformed, but for the first time I suddenly thought that perhaps I wasn't deformed enough. For the pile of shit that I felt like, I was still inordinately handsome. I turned around and punched the wall behind the couch. The lacerations on the skin of my knuckles provided a little relief.

My empty stomach grumbled, and as I headed for the refrigerator the phone rang.

It wasn't my cell but rather the landline, and I hoarsely stated my last name without thinking.

"Same name at this end," Tamara's voice answered angrily. "Have a nice sleep? How'd you do in German composition at school. Good? How good is good? Okay, then come help me."

"In a taxi?" I pulled the towel up helplessly, as if somebody was watching me.

"On a bike," said Tamara. "And bring a banana for Ferdi."

I dressed as quickly as a fireman, pulling the clean clothes over my unwashed body, repeating over and over the address Tamara had given me since I couldn't find a pen and had to just remember. "Next to the town hall, everyone knows it," she'd mumbled when I asked how to get there.

Three of the bikes in the garage had flats. Only the last one, a rusty old girl's bike, seemed to have any air in its tires. I hopped on and stepped into the pedals. I could pretty much picture where the town hall was. I would just have to ask if I had any trouble, and I sure was looking forward to that eventuality.

I passed a grocery store along the way and went in quickly and bought a kilo of bananas that I then had to balance with one hand as I rode. Fortunately it was really as simple to get there as Tamara had said. The same moment I saw the town hall I also saw the name of the local paper on a building a few doors down. I parked the rusty monster at the bike stand and, armed with the bananas, ran inside. Based on the sound of Tamara's voice, it was something of an emergency.

She was sitting with two men at a round worn table and fighting with them about some pieces of paper over which they were all bent. Behind them stretched a large room full of people all talking on the phone. As I got closer I could see that lying in front of Tamara there were lots of designs in square black frames. Inside the thick frames were images of cut roses, lit candles, broken hearts, intertwined crosses, piles of stones. Photos of forests and lakes. And on each of these printouts I saw my last name, and then my eye fell on the first name of my father.

"What do you think, Marek, a photo?" asked Tamara as if we were continuing a previous conversation.

"Where's Ferdi?" I asked because I was tired of holding the bananas.

Tamara pointed behind her. He was on the floor, also bent over a piece of paper. He was drawing. Great, I thought, almost like at a grief support group.

"A photo?" she repeated impatiently.

"For god's sake, Tamara."

"What? There are so many images in the catalogue. I can't decide."

"I'd do it with no image."

"It doesn't cost any more to have one, Marek."

The two men in suits, one with glasses, one without, kept glancing back and forth between her and me.

"You could also use a photo of him, from when he was younger . . . "

"Tamara!"

"A cross is always good, but then again he wasn't religious . . . "

"I'm begging you!"

"A rose is really something more for a woman, don't you think? And candles are for old people?"

Come back, Claudia, I thought. Stop all the photos, crosses, and candles. Come up with some words for a death notice that nobody will have to be embarrassed about. Please!

But she was off in a hearse bringing home the body of her dead ex-husband. She couldn't help with the decision as to whether boughs of oak or maple would better suit my father. I had to get through it alone.

"Tamara," I said. "You're a great woman. Can I ask you something?"

She looked at me skeptically. The two men exchanged looks.

"Could you please take a walk? I'll take care of this."

She looked into my eyes. I didn't look away. "Please," I said.

She made a "pfff" sound and then rushed out of the room like somebody was chasing her. On the faces of the two men you could see the realization that with all the trouble caused by death, the business it brought was sometimes just not worth it.

"Just a second, please," I said.

I went over to Ferdi and handed him a banana. He took it without looking up and started to peel it. He held his pen in his teeth and then spat it out to take a bite. He had a lot of hidden talents, one of which was being able to eat a banana at warp speed. At least he was getting some vitamins and magnesium, I thought. Mourning over cream of wheat alone wasn't enough.

I was a little reluctant to give him the third one.

"First you have to help me, Ferdi," I said. "I can see that you draw really well. Can you make a picture of your papa? And my papa. Then you can have all of the bananas that are left."

For dinner, Tamara had bought sausages and was roasting potatoes. She had me cut cucumber for the salad. I cut the slices too thick for her liking. So I had to try to saw my way through the slices to make thinner slices. She wore an apron and acted very businesslike. Ferdi sat on a child's seat with his head resting on his arm.

"*Ne spi*, Ferdi, *chas budem kushat*," said Tamara to Ferdi. He didn't react.

"Maybe he doesn't speak Ukrainian," I said.

"I can't really speak it right either," said Tamara.

"Why do you speak it then?"

"It's Russian, genius. There are a lot of Russians in the Ukraine. The child should learn my native language."

"Why?"

"Because." She put down the wooden spoon she'd been using to turn the pieces of potato and sat down on a stool. "I can't take it anymore," she said, and big teardrops started rolling down her cheeks.

I looked at her. This wet face, the tears hanging from her eyelashes. She was a little girl, no matter how old she really was. Some women stayed little girls their entire lives, others were born old. She was younger than me, even younger than Janne. And my father had left her all alone in the dark forest.

"I can't take it anymore," she said again. "I want him to come back."

"I'd get him back for you if I could."

"Oh no." She covered her face with her hands. "I'm such an idiot. I keep thinking that Claudia will come home and say they messed up in Switzerland, that it was someone else, and maybe it wasn't so bad for this other guy, maybe at least he didn't have such a young child . . . "

" . . . or such a sweet wife," I said awkwardly. I wiped the cucumber slices from the knife blade into the salad bowl, dried my fingers on my T-shirt, and put my hand on Tamara's trembling shoulder.

"Just tell me what I can do for you, I'll do anything I can."

"You're so nice." She sniffled and ran the back of her hand across her smudged face. "You're nice just like him. Can you carry Ferdi upstairs?"

Ferdi was heavy and smelled like bananas and milk. He hung in my arms like a sack, with his mouth open and his head lolling back. My heart raced. I was terribly afraid of dropping him. I wondered whether children were more unwieldy when they were asleep. I didn't know how I could get him up the stairs without stumbling and falling.

"Should I take him?" asked Tamara.

"No," I said, pressing the word out between my teeth. "Just turn the lights on in the staircase."

Step by step I climbed, with Ferdi's breath on my neck, the smell of his moist sweaty hair in my nose, a scent that reminded me of rye bread, the moist skin under his T-shirt that made me afraid he might slip out of my hands. I thought of my father: I'd never been hiking in the mountains. Maybe this was what it was like to scale the top of a mountain, and when you fell it was all over.

We made it, and Tamara had opened Ferdi's door for me and switched on the night-light that bathed the room in red light.

She pulled back the covers and I laid Ferdi on the bed and

kneeled down next to him. I had probably taken fifteen minutes to get up the stairs. Tamara pulled off Ferdi's pants until he was lying there with long skinny bare legs and his dinosaur underpants, then she unrolled his slipper-socks from his feet and he murmured something and opened his eyes. He looked right at me and I wished he hadn't because I figured the boy would get the shock of his life and would still be sleeping with a night-light at forty; he would never be able to take his kids to a haunted house, and . . . but it was too late for me to step away into the darkness. I wasn't even standing, I was kneeling.

Ferdi looked at me with his eyes wide open and smiled.

H e wasn't really awake," said Tamara. "He often talks in his sleep and even walks around sometimes, he's, what's the word, moonstruck."

It occurred to me that I used to do the same. "I used to sleepwalk when I was little, too," I said. "Claudia used to lock the front door and hide the knives and scissors from me."

Tamara looked sideways at me with concern on her face.

We'd gone back down to the kitchen, finished making the food, and sat down opposite each other. The silence was palpable. I tried to avoid glancing at her so as not to have to think about what had happened that morning. Now, with Ferdi not there with us, the image kept reappearing in my smoldering brain.

Tamara got up for the fifth time to get something else out of the cabinet. This time it was a bottle of vodka and two glasses which she put down between us on the table.

"We haven't raised a glass to him," she said.

"Hmm?" I turned the bottle toward myself and studied the label as if I might recognize something from it.

"Are you even allowed?" she asked worriedly. "You're already sixteen, right?"

"If I'm allowed to fuck you, I'm allowed to drink vodka with you," I said, and she put her hand over my mouth.

"I never want to hear that again."

She poured vodka, a small glass for herself and a tiny bit for me, and then stood up. I followed her lead. She lifted her glass and closed her eyes. Her lips moved, then she put the glass to her mouth. I sipped at mine as she opened her eyes and put her glass back down.

"Claudia," she said.

I heard it now, too. The engine, which got louder as it pulled away, the footsteps on the front steps, the key turning in the lock. Claudia stood in the doorway and waved. At first I thought she was hurt but then I realized she was just horribly tired. I went over to her in order to brace her, but she pulled her arm away from me.

"And?" Tamara turned up next to her on the other side. "It's not him, right?"

"Yes it is," said Claudia with her eyes closed.

It was an endless night. Claudia sat at the kitchen table, and a long snaking line of coffee cups began to form in front of her. She took a sip and put the cup aside; after a few minutes it was cold so I made her a new cup. I was afraid she might fall off her chair. I kept thinking I was looking at a strange woman in a Claudia costume sitting there, and I wanted to shake her and scream at her to give me back my mother.

She didn't tell us anything. Tamara sat opposite Claudia, fiddled with the handles of the coffee cups, and asked questions that turned my stomach. I didn't want to think about how they must have made Claudia feel. She wanted to know what he looked like, whether he looked peaceful, whether he was naked, whether he had a tag on his big toe the way they do on TV, and whether his injuries were visible. Claudia just kept shaking her head like she was trying to fend off a fly, but Tamara wouldn't stop until I finally hit the table with my fist and yelled, "SHUT UP!"

Tamara blinked at me with shock out of her tear-filled eyes and Claudia put her hand on my forearm, but she was so weak her hand slumped back to the table. "Don't yell at her."

I kept looking back and forth between the two of them.

"Take her to bed," said Claudia blankly.

I stood up obediently and offered Tamara my arm. I had expected her to protest, but she let me help her up and, sniffling like an old woman, went up the stairs by my side. I accompanied her to the door of the bedroom and stood there indecisively. Tamara put her arm around my neck and kissed my nose. I tried to return the kiss and my lips slipped across her salty cheek, then she let go and disappeared behind the door.

I stood there for a while and listened to the noises that she made, the rushing water in the shower, the shuffling steps across the room; only after I heard the mattress squeak beneath her did I go back downstairs to Claudia.

She was sitting in the same position that I'd left her in, and was rolling a cigarette in her fingers. I grabbed a pack of matches from the kitchen and struck one. She took a deep drag on the cigarette, then coughed and put it out in one of the coffee cups. It sizzled. Claudia's face was reddened and there were tears in her eyes, but maybe it was from coughing.

I put my hands on her shoulders and was alarmed at how small and fragile she felt. From above I looked at the top of her head, the gray hair that was coming in beneath the honey blonde.

"Mama," I said. "Please go to bed."

She shook her head and pointed at the chair next to her. I let myself drop onto the chair. She took my hand, her fingers were cold and shaking.

"Did you at least sleep in the car?"

She shook her head again.

"Everyone was very nice," she said. "The funeral director called the police from the road to let them know we would be there soon and they had everything prepared. I just had to go in for a second and say, yes that's him. I recognized him immediately. He looked like he was sleeping. He had a scrape on his forehead and was very cold."

I squeezed her hand.

"I'm happy that I saw him," she said. "I'm happy that he's here now. I'm happy that he looks good. I feel better as a result."

I nodded as if I believed her.

"You have to tell Tammy," said Claudia. "She's the widow, she has a right to know what it was like. But I just can't talk about it with her." I squeezed her hand again, which was supposed to signal my consent. "I know that it's hard for you, but I beg you."

I shook my head to make clear that it wasn't hard for me. I couldn't get out any words. And I was also incredibly tired, and outside it was getting light again.

Then Claudia laid her head on her crossed arms and began to sob.

I was dreaming of Marlon when someone shook me. I opened my eyes and saw Claudia, not the Claudia from yesterday but the one I was used to. She'd gone outside the natural contours of her lips with her lipstick again.

"Get up, it's already ten," she said. I swallowed the remark I wanted to make about having spent the whole night awake. Something told me that Claudia wouldn't be moved by it.

"Tammy and Ferdi are awake already, too."

"And?"

"Your father is dead."

I didn't say that he still would be two hours from now. Since I'd felt her shoulders yesterday and seen the gray roots of her hair, I'd had no desire to play the smartass anymore. I was more likely to offer her a comfy chair and a warm blanket for her legs.

"Where is Dirk, by the way?" I asked.

"Dirk has to work. He's coming to the funeral," she said in an even tone.

"Great," I said.

"I think so, too," she said.

When I went downstairs they were all sitting at the breakfast table. Tammy was wearing jeans and a tight T-shirt and had her still-wet hair pulled back in a ponytail. She looked somehow recharged. Claudia reported that Tammy had gotten up very early and gone shopping for breakfast, bread and butter, cheese and milk, honey and jam, and most important of all, a copy of the local paper. She listed every detail as if Tammy was a crippled kid who had ridden the bus alone for the first time.

"Very well done, Tammy," I said.

"What the hell is this?" She slammed the open newspaper down in front of me.

I slowly took a sip of coffee then looked at the paper.

"That's the death notice that you asked me to take care of."

Claudia stretched out her neck interestedly.

"What kind of sick picture is this?" hissed Tammy.

"I made it," said Ferdi.

"I can't blame the child for drawing stick figures, but you are not six years old, Marek, you must have at least an ounce of sense under those slick curls."

I feigned confusion and pulled at my hair. I'd never had curls, my hair just got a little wavy when it was long. It had grown back a bit since Johanna had cut it with the kitchen shears.

"Those candles, crosses, and roses are awful," I said. "If you had an ounce of taste you would have realized that immediately."

"If you had an ounce of sense you wouldn't have run a stick-figure portrait of your father in his death notice," screamed Tammy at a volume that assaulted my eardrums and my entire nervous system. I needed to hide in a soundproof underground bunker.

"And why is it all white against a black background? Is that a screw-up? A printing error? Or maybe you should have taken your sunglasses off for once so you could have seen the difference?"

"Everybody has black on white," I said.

"Exactly."

"I wanted something different. The other way around. It's a death notice, what's so bad about a black background?"

"How am I supposed to leave the house and look people in the eye after a death notice like this? How is Ferdi supposed to go to kindergarten when all the parents of his friends have seen this? And with my name at the bottom?"

"I couldn't exactly leave you off—you happen to be the widow. All of our names are there."

"You'll be gone in a few days and will never come back. I have to survive in this hole, you've ruined my reputation!" The first few words Tammy had said calmly but by the end she was screaming again.

"If you're so worried about your reputation maybe for once you should wear a top that covers your tits," I shouted back. Claudia had been sitting there motionless, listening, but now she winced and I realized I'd gone too far.

"Forgive me, Tammy, that really has nothing to do with this," I said quickly. "Your clothes and your figure are really incredibly nice, and you really did a great job shopping for breakfast."

"Just shut up, Marek," said Claudia.

She reached out and plucked the paper off the table. She spread it out in front of her and studied it for several minutes.

"I got the details of the funeral from Tammy, in case there's a mistake," I said hurriedly.

"There's no mistake with *that* part, you coward," said Tammy disdainfully.

"I think it's okay," said Claudia finally. "It is indeed . . . somewhat unconventional. But I can imagine that he would have liked it. And most of all because of your beautiful picture, Ferdi."

Ferdi smiled at her shyly over the rim of his bowl of cream of wheat.

The next thing Tammy said at the breakfast table was that she too wanted to see my father.

"Really?" I asked with my mouth full. "Why?"

"To say goodbye, you idiot."

"That's normal in her culture. Saying goodbye at an open coffin," said Claudia to me quietly, though of course Tammy heard her as well.

"How else would you do it?" she asked. "Ferdi needs to see him, too."

I thought I had misheard her. Claudia looked just as confused. Ferdi was sweetening his cream of wheat with several spoonfuls of Nutella and mixing it all up thoroughly. Then he scooped the brown goop into his mouth, the edges of which still seemed to be smeared from yesterday.

"Are you sure?" asked Claudia weakly.

"He'll never see him again." Tammy turned to her son. "Ferdi, *hochesh uvidet papu*?"

Ferdi nodded without looking up.

"What was that?" I asked skeptically.

"We just settled it," said Tammy. Ever since we'd slept together I seemed to be nothing but irritating to her. Maybe I had acted particularly idiotic.

"Don't you think it might be traumatic for a child?"

"What?" asked Tammy.

"I can't fight anymore," sighed Claudia. "Otherwise I'm not going to get through all of this."

I looked at her. Then we agreed very quickly that I should accompany Tammy and Ferdi to the funeral home. That is, Claudia asked me pleadingly whether I would do it and I said yes. She mumbled that somebody had to be there for the child, and Tammy could hardly be asked to handle it given the situation. I looked at Claudia and knew that I couldn't ask her to handle it for me. Those days were over.

"You don't have to come if you're afraid," said Tammy scornfully as she stood in front of the mirror in the hall and put on her eyeliner.

I didn't feel like fighting with her anymore, I even held back from saying that *he* could no longer see her makeup. I just said, "He's my father too," and wondered silently why Ferdi's pants pockets were bulging out. Ferdi stood there concentrating, his eyes not looking at anything in particular, and waited while Tammy undid her ponytail and then put it back up exactly the same way.

On the street she linked arms with me and took Ferdi's hand with her other arm. I still hadn't gotten used to the fact that you could go everywhere on foot here, buy bananas, go to the newspaper office, the funeral home, everything was just around the corner. I looked at Tammy's profile. We had to keep stopping so Tammy could accept condolences from other residents as we passed. Some chased her down the street in order to hug her and say a few words about my father. Tammy looked fragile but dignified. Ferdi switched to holding my hand so Tammy had hers free to shake other people's hands. After she'd thanked each person she introduced me extremely solemnly, and then I shook hands and mumbled thanks and then considerately turned away as their gazes dropped so fast you'd think they had dropped a fifty euro note on the sidewalk and they yanked their hand out of mine.

I certainly didn't object to the fact that we were stopped so frequently. I was definitely in no hurry. But at some point we arrived anyway. I immediately remembered the place, which was housed in an old timbered house. I often stopped in front of it as a child and looked at the changing seasonal window displays. The prettiest display was always before Christmas, when the urns would be sitting on cotton balls and have fake snow on them, blue crystal stars glittered on the pine branches, and everything looked so festive that at five years old I had asked Claudia if we couldn't set up a similarly beautiful display in my room.

But now it was October, and the window display was some kind of harvest theme, with chestnuts, apples, corncobs, and fluttering red and yellow maple leaves hanging from nearly invisible strings. I wondered how they would decorate for Halloween.

Tammy's hand trembled in the crook of my arm and I let go of Ferdi for a second and covered her fingers with my other hand. Her thick gold wedding ring had been warmed by the sun. She stood still, so did I. Minutes passed.

She pulled her hand away and entered the door ahead of us.

B ehind the timbered façade was a square paved yard where several cars were parked, including a hearse. Two child-sized angels stood watch over the entrance to a low-rise building behind. The funeral director was waiting there.

"Everything is ready," he said and held Tammy's hand for quite a long time.

She nodded and looked at the door that he stepped aside to allow her to approach. I stared at her. Then I squeezed Ferdi's hand so hard that he said, "Ouch!"

"Will you all go in together?" asked the funeral director.

No, I wanted to scream. I don't want to go in at all, and as far as I'm concerned I don't think Ferdi should either. I don't want to be even partially responsible for another source of life-long pain for the boy. I didn't put any stock in East European social conventions about kissing corpses. Please get me out of here.

But Tammy looked up at me with her eyes wide open.

"I'll go first," I said.

"Together," she sighed.

The funeral director held the door for us. Ferdi squealed again from the squeeze of my hand. The scent of melted wax hit us. I realized that I'd been holding my breath.

Now we were inside. The funeral director closed the door. I turned around for a second, he was waiting at the exit with his hands folded and his eyes down.

I looked forward again and would like to have screamed.

Against the far wall was an open coffin. A man was sleeping there. Obviously I knew this man was my father and that he wasn't sleeping. I tried to move toward him but my legs wouldn't respond.

There was a click behind me and the sound of an organ filled the room. My father was lying in a coffin, he was dead, deader than dead, he would never be able to get up again. And yet he was just as I remembered him. Like a perfect replica, a wax figure. In all the years I hadn't succeeded in forgetting him.

But I had forgotten Ferdi. He was no longer holding my hand. I turned around. He was standing next to the funeral director, watching me. Tammy was collapsed in the corner.

"Come, Ferdi," I said. "We'll go back out."

He was at my side in a flash. I took his fingers, which were warm and sweaty and slipped trustingly into my hand. Together with him I could keep my feet under me. He pulled me forward adamantly, and I couldn't do anything but follow him. He stood on his tiptoes and looked into the coffin. Then he let go of my hand to touch the lace blanket with which our father was covered to his waist. The blanket shifted.

"Ferdi," I whispered, shocked.

"What is that?" He pointed with his little pointer finger at the scrape that our father had on his forehead. His finger hung in the air above the face, then it sunk and touched the skin for a moment.

"Cold," said Ferdi.

"He hurt himself, but he can't feel it anymore," I mumbled. The longer I stood there, the more at ease I became. I no longer wanted to scream and run away. I looked down at the body of my father. He had on a suit, a white shirt, a white tie, that's the way he always went to court and he put his robe on over that outfit. The tie was crooked. Without realizing what I was doing I reached out my hand and straightened it.

Ferdi walked around the coffin. His fingers ran across our father's face again. Then without warning he stuck his finger into our father's ear.

"Careful," I whispered, but he ignored me. He walked a few more times around the coffin. His hands ran along the edge.

"It's just a box, Ferdi." I had the stupid feeling I needed to say something. Not for him, more for me to know that I could still speak. My voice, dulled by the organ music, sounded strange to me. He nodded; he could see it all himself. Then he stuck his hands in his pants pockets and pulled out several matchbox cars and a couple of already squishy chocolate bars. He parked the cars along his father's tie; one fell, Ferdi rummaged around in the coffin to find it and pulled it out again.

"Ferdi, *perestan*!" Tammy had gotten herself together and was now standing next to us. I took a step to the side to let her in at the head of the coffin. She was trembling so badly that the floor beneath us seemed to shake. Everything trembled with her. I put my arm around her shoulders and squeezed her to stop her from shaking so much. She reached out a hand and touched the stubble on the dead face. She drew her hand right back, surprised by the coldness. Then she shook off my arm and threw herself onto my father's chest.

She sobbed so loudly that I was afraid something might break inside her. I turned for a second toward the funeral director. He had left the room. I didn't hear the awful music anymore, either. My young stepmother kissed the face of my dead father, and two feelings welled up in me that I did not know well. One was awe, and it filled me so thoroughly that I thought I might burst. The other was envy.

Tammy grew quiet and lay there with her head on the pillow, her cheek against his. Then she got up, wiped the tears from her face, and began to straighten up the blanket.

"Does he have shoes on?" Ferdi showed the persistence of

a young scientist in trying to figure out a way to get a peek under the foot-end of the blanket.

"*Perestan*," said Tamara. Suddenly it occurred to me that my father might be covered that way because the funeral director hadn't clothed him below the waist, and I pulled Ferdi away from his feet.

"Why does he have his hands like that?" Ferdi fidgeted with his folded hands.

"He can sleep better that way." Tammy's voice wafted tenderly through the room.

"I don't think so." Ferdi tried to unfold the hands. And instead of barking at him Tammy suddenly started to help him.

"Come on, help us," she said over her shoulder to me.

"No," I said with the same resolve in my voice that I felt inside myself. I was afraid they would break something. I had no idea why I ended up helping them after all. It was futile, though: the hands were permanently wedged together, hard and cold, and suddenly I shouted. It felt like a finger had moved.

"What are you screaming for?" Tammy began to pull on the forearm, concentrating. Ferdi helped from the other side.

"I think he moved."

She threw her head back and laughed. It echoed through the room.

"Ferdi, I don't think we're going to manage it," she said. "We'll leave him this way. It's fine this way."

Ferdi hung his arms dejectedly.

I had no idea how much time had elapsed. The door had opened and closed a few times. Tammy kissed my father a few more times and the smacks filled the room.

"Ferdi, do you want to as well?" she asked.

He nodded and I lifted him up. He touched the dead cheek with his lips. I put him back down. Christ, I thought, he's only six.

"And now you." Tammy poked me in the back.

"I don't want to," I said. I had long since crossed the line of what was possible for me. I wasn't planning to stray any further beyond it.

"You have to."

"I do not have to do anything."

"You'll feel better afterwards, I promise." Tammy's hand was still resting between my shoulder blades. I could feel its heat through my T-shirt. The room was cold.

To get her to stop, I bent down over the coffin. I wasn't planning to kiss my father. I was afraid to. But the tip of my nose touched his and didn't fall off, so I moved a little higher and felt his marble forehead beneath my lips. I couldn't remember the last kiss he had given me.

I straightened back up with my eyes closed. It was burning beneath my eyelids.

Tammy handed me the sunglasses, which had fallen into the coffin when I leaned down. She took my hand and with her other hand held Ferdi's. We stood for a moment in the doorway and all turned around together. My father lay in a coffin, next to him burned a meter-high white candle, and I thought that it was now time to leave him behind forever. Ferdi craned his neck to look at him even after we had passed through the door and were back in the sun. He kept turning around until the door closed. The funeral director was waiting next to a stone angel with his hands crossed and considerately avoided looking us in the eyes.

We took our leave and left. It was very warm, the sun shone down from above, through the crack between my glasses and my forehead and onto my eyelids; my feet bounced along the asphalt, and I realized to my surprise that Tammy had been right. I felt a lightness of heart that I hadn't felt in a long time.

Claudia said I didn't need a black suit. Tammy claimed the opposite.

"You'd look so sweet," she said, ignoring Claudia's scolding look. "How often does your father die?"

"He is still a boy." Claudia sounded like a worn-out general who just wanted to win one last battle before collapsing. "He doesn't need some silly suit. He can wear black jeans."

"He's a man." Tammy tussled my hair. "Ferdi is a man, too. He's also getting a suit."

Claudia sighed. Now she was acting the way you expect an ex-wife to act around her successor. She was annoyed. She rolled her eyes. I figured she was out of energy. That she hadn't been like this up to now was an act of self-restraint for which she wasn't getting as much credit as she deserved.

"It'll be over soon," she said and leaned back with her eyes closed after Tammy rushed out to the garage and started furiously sorting some garbage bags or other as if there was nothing more important in the world to do. "Things will be better after the funeral."

"Why?" I asked.

She shrugged her shoulders. "It always is."

"It's no problem for me to wear a suit. I don't have any black jeans."

We went shopping, Claudia and I, the two of us, as if I were Ferdi's age. There weren't a lot of options. The shop at the southern end of the market square sold only plus sizes, the one on the northern side everything from toothpicks to underpants, but no trousers. In the last possibility, a boutique catering to Eastern Europeans, I tried on a suit. "We could drive to Frankfurt," Claudia had suggested, but I just waved the idea aside.

"Claudia," I said quietly when I came out of the changing room. She was waiting with her eyes closed, sitting on a stool and leaning against the wall. I said her name again but she didn't react. At first I thought she'd had a stroke but she had just fallen asleep.

I exhaled and ran my hand across my face. Claudia opened her eyes and smiled.

"You look good," she said.

"Thanks. Fits well, too."

"No, really, everything together looks great. Look at yourself." She pointed to a tall mirror and looked me in the eyes.

"No, thanks," I said.

Her face winced as if I had stepped with my full weight on her foot.

"Sorry, Claudia, but I'm not going to do it," I said. "I never want to see myself again. Do you understand—never. You shouldn't bother asking. I'm fine with it. I'm living a fulfilled life, I'm burying my father, buying myself a suit, I even keep finding girls who are willing to try to be with me despite my face. I am a fundamentally happy person, so now please stop trying to remind me of my glorious past. It's over. It bothers you more than me."

She nodded and looked down at her hands.

I went back into the changing room and pulled my phone out of the pocket of my pants. I looked at it hundreds of times per day. Janne hadn't called. By now I knew she wasn't going to, but I was waiting for it all the same.

My mama is coming," said Tammy when we got back to the house, me with my shopping bag in my hand and Claudia with a fan she'd bought at the ninety-nine cent shop on the market square. She was fanning herself and breathing hard even though it wasn't very hot. I was worried about her blood pressure.

"She's coming to the funeral." Tammy kept talking even when neither Claudia nor I paid her announcement sufficient attention. "She's arriving tonight."

"Good that you told us," said Claudia flatly. "Is she coming on her own?"

"What do you think? The flights are expensive, you know."

"That's very nice of her to come," I said cautiously.

Tammy looked at me as if I had said something incredibly moronic.

"What?" I asked.

"It's her son-in-law, you know."

"Had she ever met him?"

"No."

"Don't get bent out of shape," said Claudia. "Of course Tammy is paying for the plane ticket, but it doesn't affect your inheritance."

"Don't be ridiculous, it's got nothing to do with that."

"Then what is it?"

I couldn't explain it. Somehow, in a highly roundabout way,

everything had to do to Janne in the end. But I wouldn't have said that even under threat of execution.

"I don't need any more people gaping at me," I said.

Claudia shrugged. "Funerals, birthdays, and weddings have been public events since the dawn of time. There's no point in fighting it. Get yourself together."

I had no idea she could be so harsh.

My father's Ukrainian mother-in-law was supposed to land just after midnight.

"You have a driver's license?" I asked Tamara incredulously when she started looking for the car keys while continuously checking the flight information on her phone. Then I recalled that a week ago Tamara had probably been totally capable of dealing with life. It was unlikely that my father had led her around by the hand and taken care of everything for her. Even if she was his beloved little girl with the big breasts. Somebody still had to defend the murderers and rapists and earn the money for new garden sculptures.

"Unlike you," she said haughtily. "Will you get your license when you turn seventeen?"

"Go to the airport with her, Marek," ordered Claudia in a voice that permitted no objections.

"And what if I say no?"

"Just do it, Marek," said Tammy. "If I drive into a tree Claudia will be rid of us both."

I couldn't figure out what had happened. Why the atmosphere had taken such a nosedive and we were no longer a happy grieving family like we had been when I arrived. Why Tammy and Claudia suddenly had to attack each other. An hour earlier they'd been at each other's throats about the funeral arrangements. Tammy rejected Claudia's classical music playlist on the grounds that it was old men's music. She waved two strange-looking CDs and had another one tucked under her arm.

"He *was* an old man!" said Claudia, using every ounce of her strength to control herself. "He was an old man, and there will be a lot of other old men at his funeral. Colleagues, clients, the mayor for god's sake."

"So? It's not their funeral."

Claudia groaned.

In the end she won out on the music front. But that meant Tamara got her way with the reception.

"We're going to invite everyone here." She spread her arms out as if she was trying to hug the whole house. "There's plenty of room here." And this is my fiefdom and I am in charge here, that's what it said across her nearly flawless forehead, blemished only by a barely visible worry-crease.

"And the coffee cake? And the coffee?" Claudia looked away as if it was more than she could handle to have to look Tammy in the eye. "Who will you put in charge of that?"

"Nobody," said Tammy. "I'll make it all myself. With Mama."

"For two hundred people?"

"For a thousand for all I care."

"Why are you guys fighting so much?" I asked in the car. I noticed that Tammy had painted her nails black today. She drove like a crazy person and I double-checked several times to make sure I had my seat belt on. I still had my whole life ahead of me. "I mean, up to now it's been all peace and love and pancakes between you. You were so nice to each other."

"What?" She hadn't been listening to me.

"Don't give my mother such a hard time, Tammy, she's at the end of her rope," I said a bit louder.

She bit her lip.

"I know that things aren't so easy for you either," I said diplomatically.

She turned her face toward the window. Given that she was going 120 miles per hour it was a bit worrisome.

"Keep your eyes on the road, I don't want have an accident."

"It's not like you could get much worse," she said.

"Go ahead and speak your mind, I don't care."

She turned her face back toward me. There were tears in her eyes and I couldn't understand what the source of the tears could be. Her mother was arriving, was that a reason to cry?

"I'm sorry," I said even though she was really the one who should have been saying that. "Why hasn't your mother ever been here?"

Tamara didn't say anything.

"Not even for the wedding?"

"It was a small wedding," she mumbled.

"Why?"

"Because."

I sighed. This conversation was nothing but a minefield. For the first time it dawned on me that Tammy's faraway relatives might not have been as happy as I'd always assumed about her sudden pregnancy by the father of her host family. My father and Tammy had married immediately so she wouldn't have to go back the Ukraine. Maybe my father wasn't so thrilled about the whole thing either. Maybe he hadn't fallen madly in love, maybe he was just doing what he saw as his duty. Maybe everything had been totally different than I had always pictured.

"I went to see my family in the Ukraine twice with Ferdi," said Tammy.

"Does your mother know, by the way?"

"Know what? That he's dead? Of course, that's why she's coming."

"Know this." I drew a circle around my face with my hands.

"Oh," said Tammy. "Don't worry about it. The world doesn't revolve around your pimples. She's definitely seen worse."

We waited in front of the arrivals board at Frankfurt airport. My head hurt from leaning back the whole time. Tammy had snuggled up to me and laid her head on my shoulder.

"I wouldn't do that," I said.

"Why not?"

"Out of respect and whatnot."

"Respect for who?" She kissed me on the cheek and then again on the neck.

"You're a widow, Tammy."

"Exactly."

"So stop kissing me."

"You're like a brother to me." She kissed me on the ear, and it sounded loud. "Like a cousin," she corrected. "Without you I'd have completely lost it by now."

She was talking like she was drunk. It even seemed as if she couldn't stand up straight. I was propping her up. Her waist was very thin, I could get one arm all the way around it. For a second I noticed that she smelled like peonies behind her ears. Then she shoved me away with both hands and tried to steady herself on her own. She stepped on my foot with her heel but I didn't make a sound.

"Mama," she cried shrilly and stumbled off.

I had expected Tammy's mother to be like her, long legs, long hair, just twice her age. Or, perhaps less likely, a little round woman with a long coat and a headscarf like I'd seen a long time ago in an article on Kiev in *National Geographic*. The last thing I had expected was that Tammy's mother would look like a copy of Claudia, tall, disheveled hair that wasn't blonde but red—Claudia had dyed hers the same shade a few years back. Tammy's mother was wearing flashy glasses and had a large mouth. And she spoke English better than me.

"My mother is a professor, you idiot," hissed Tammy in my ear as I pulled her suspiciously heavy suitcase along. I'd tried to compliment the newly arrived mother on her English.

"You could have told me," I hissed back at her. "You don't look anything like her!"

"Thank god."

Somehow I now understood why Tammy and Claudia couldn't stand each other anymore. I liked her mother. She introduced herself as Evgenija, the Russian version of Eugenia, and said her foreign colleagues called her Jenny.

I liked the firm handshake that accompanied the English words I took for her expression of condolences. I liked her accent, which I would have liked to have myself. I liked the limited level of interest she showed as she looked fleetingly at my face before turning to her daughter. And I liked the way Tammy suddenly changed in her company. The tension melted from her body, she slumped comfortably at the steering wheel, her back curved, her shoulders drooped, and she talked quietly with her mother and the gurgle of their conversation sounded to me like wind chimes or the distant whoosh of the ocean. I relaxed in the backseat and kept dozing off. Now and then I opened an eye and caught Tammy's gaze in the rearview mirror.

"By the day after tomorrow we'll have gotten through everything," said Claudia. She wasn't able to get up to say hello because Ferdi was asleep in her lap and Tammy's mother had vehemently insisted that the child's well-being came first. She ran her hand across Ferdi's sweaty head. The dispassion of this Ukrainian granny surprised me. Of course we were the same way, but I had expected far more emotion from her. I had the feeling that there was a question in the look she gave Tammy after looking at Ferdi: *Is he really yours?*

Now Tammy and her mother had disappeared upstairs to requisition another room, and Claudia was still sitting there while my little brother made rasping noises in his sleep. Claudia's eyes kept closing, too, but she kept jerking awake.

"She's nice, isn't she?" she mumbled as her eyelids fluttered.

"Mama Evgenija? Absolutely delightful," I said.

"The day after tomorrow," whispered Claudia. "Everything will be over the day after tomorrow."

A t eight in the morning my phone rang. I sat up, reached out and accidentally knocked it off the nightstand, and then slid to the floor to try to pick it up. It blinked and jumped around, vibrating. I chased after it like a stork after a toad. Maybe I had gone completely nuts, which would mean I was adapting to my environment. But then I caught it and it was still ringing and I pressed it to my ear. I didn't recognize the number in the display but I knew who it was.

I was wrong. It wasn't Janne, it wasn't anyone from the cripple troop. It was Lucy.

I recognized her even before she said her name. I'd deleted her number along with all the others, but the sound of her voice took me back for a second to a time that no longer existed to me. I felt the corners of my mouth forming a smile. But it withered away just as soon as Lucy haltingly offered her condolences. She sounded throaty, as if she had spent hours crying out of a false sense of solidarity.

"Thanks," I said. "It's very nice of you to think of me."

"I'm happy that I finally managed to reach you," she said. I waited. I was less inclined than ever to discuss my conduct over the past year. She wasn't stupid and understood that on her own.

"How are you, Marek?" she asked, her voice clear again, light and clear, and I could tell that one false word or a false tone would cause her to break down in tears again. I sniffed the tipping point of a nervous breakdown. Not that she was the type to fall apart, but she had her limits, and apparently I still knew her well enough to know where they were.

"How did you find out . . . " I asked.

It was simple. She had called our house to try to catch up with me. She had spoken on the answering machine and a very nice man named Dirk had heard the message. He called her back, told her everything, and encouraged her to reach out to me, because in a situation like this I could surely use words of support from a dear old friend.

"Idiot," I said.

She laughed. "No," she said. "He just doesn't know you very well yet."

"You can drop the 'yet.'" I said.

She said nothing and I was happy she didn't try to engage in banter. She asked about my father, held her breath as I told her about him falling off the mountain and breaking his neck, and I heard her gulp loudly several times as I told her about viewing the open coffin. I was happy to be able to tell someone about it.

"I had no idea you had a little brother," she said after a pause.

"I didn't really."

"But now you do."

"Now I do," I agreed halfheartedly.

"Can I come to the funeral?"

"No," I said quickly. "Definitely not. You didn't even know him, my father I mean." I kept talking quickly since she wasn't saying anything. "It's a hole, this town where I grew up. Everything is weird here. My stepmother is a ridiculously young Ukrainian girl, and Claudia is slowly going crazy, and so am I . . . "

"I'd love to help," said Lucy. "At the very least I could babysit or something. Is your little brother a sweetheart?"

"A total sweetheart." Suddenly I got angry at her. I couldn't believe she was using the circumstances to slime her way back into my life. She'd found a moment of weakness, a moment when I had the feeling that things could perhaps be like they used to be. I thought it was insidious, and if anyone had said she meant well it would have just made me angrier.

"He's very sweet, but you're never going to babysit him, Lucy." I heard the way she was taken aback by my change in tone—she hadn't reckoned with such a rejection after I'd sounded so promisingly open, *almost like it used to be*. I could sense how her breathing changed at the other end of the line. I didn't think she deserved any better.

"Don't you understand that I feel guilty," came blurting out of her. "Can't you get it through your head that I was there, too? That nothing will ever be the same for me either?"

"Don't talk nonsense," I said wearily. She'd already made this case in countless tiresome letters. I didn't need her feelings of guilt. I didn't have any choice then and couldn't do anything differently now. "I didn't step between you and the animal because I'm so unbelievably chivalrous," I said. "You can call me a superhero for all I care, but just bear in mind that I never was one. You're confusing me with somebody else. It was first and foremost a reflex, and secondly an accident. I was shitting myself and often wished afterwards that I hadn't done it, in which case it would have been you instead of me. That's why I don't want to talk to you, Lucy. I don't want to have to keep thinking over and over again about deciding between my face and my honor."

I didn't hear her crying, but I knew she was, and it pissed me off.

"I've told you once and for all that I don't want to see you anymore," I said. "Never again. It's nothing to do with you, I just don't want to see anyone. I don't exist anymore, get used to it. My other friends already have. Don't call me anymore and have a nice life."

She hung up without answering and I threw the phone against the wall. It popped apart into two pieces, the battery fell out. I shoved all the pieces under the bed and lay back down under the covers. Then I thought of Janne again. I would have talked to Janne because she was different from Lucy. She didn't come from the world of the undamaged. She was marked like me. You didn't have to explain things to her. I wanted to talk to her, see her, kiss her. But she didn't call. Maybe she was trying at this very moment and couldn't reach me. I got up again, put my phone back together, and turned it on. But it didn't ring.

There's going to be a Ukrainian funeral reception," said Claudia to me when, a little later, I came downstairs staggering slightly as if I were drunk. I sat down on the couch, put my feet up on the ugly two-level glass side table, and listened to the menu. Chicken soup, pierogis with fish, some slimy oatmeal kind of thing, and a never-ending supply of vodka.

"Very nice," I said.

"It's heartwarming," said Claudia. "They have written a shopping list and are off to buy everything in a few minutes. I thought perhaps you would like to accompany them and help them carry everything."

"Nothing I would rather do," I said, taking my feet off the table. Then I exploded. "Why would you say that, *perhaps you would like to accompany them*? I don't have the slightest desire to, and you know that. If you want to ask me, if you expect it of me and insist on it, then put it that way. I'm sick of all the sugarcoating."

"It's the downside of functioning in polite society," said Claudia unmoved. "To give you another example, I'd love to smack you right now but I'm not going to do so out of the same considerations."

"Me? Smack me? Why?"

"Because your self-absorption and that look on your face that says I'm-so-superior-and-sick-of-it-all gets on my nerves," said Claudia flatly.

"That's not the look on my face, it's just the way it was sewn together."

"Don't talk to me about your face," said Claudia. "I know it a lot better than you at this point."

We had to break off the conversation because Evgenija popped in with the shopping list, the length of which made me woozy. She sat down with Claudia and they both went over the list and conferred about a few items. I listened to them in amazement. They really looked like sisters. And what exasperated Claudia about Tammy's plan yesterday was no longer an issue today. The reception didn't seem to bother her at all even though yesterday she'd said that normal people in Swinehausen hired a caterer, a specific caterer, one who had specialized in such things for generations. The town was aging, lots of people died regularly, and if you wanted to belong you didn't break ranks when it came to the funeral arrangements. Now Claudia voiced nothing but enthusiasm for putting together the food, and she seemed to be sincere—I recognized the tone of her voice.

Must be a generational thing, I thought as I saw Tammy coming down the stairs with Ferdi on her back.

"You're coming shopping with us?" she asked instead of a greeting.

"Good morning to you, too, dear stepmother," I said. An inopportune thought occurred to me at that moment, about how insistent my father was about sticking to certain rules when I was young, including the importance of greetings and goodbyes and all sorts of common courtesies, and also of washing your hands.

She frowned at me. At least her mother looked like a woman with a good sense of humor, I thought, and suddenly I realized I would never have to worry about Claudia. A funny woman would never be alone. No matter what happened, you never had to worry about a funny woman. Someone would always want a woman like that. And as time passed the way she looked was less and less important.

I thought of Janne, who hadn't betrayed any particularly distinguished sense of humor up to now. I didn't want to think about how funny a man would have to be to deflect attention from his face.

I carried shopping bags—frozen salmon that had thawed out during the drive and was now dripping on the flagstones, buckwheat, packets of millet, a year's supply of grain, a bunch of small bottles of clear liquid that were knocking against each other, deep-frozen berries that like the fish had also begun to drip blood-colored drops, and other foodstuffs that I didn't recognize but that were inconceivably heavy. When I tried to say that I couldn't carry twenty full bags in one go, Tammy looked me up and down and said, "Are you a man or what? Your father . . . "

" . . . is dead," I interrupted. "Maybe he carried too many shopping . . . " At this point Tammy's mother took at least three bags from me.

I followed her with my eyes as she balanced herself on the gravel walk in her high heels. Her back was very straight and her neck looked muscular. She probably lifted weights every day.

"Did she ever hit you when you were young?" I asked Tammy.

She looked at me with Janne's disdainful look, grabbed one of the parcels from me, and followed her mother. Still heavily laden down, I shuffled toward the front door.

Inside, everything was cheerful. I caught laughter and snippets of conversation and it seemed as if a new voice had somehow emerged from one of the shopping bags. And it was an unambiguously male voice. For one crazy second I imagined that my father was back. To figure out the riddle I went on in. The bags slid off my cramped fingers. I picked them up and arranged them in an orderly row. Then I rubbed my hands, straightened my glasses, and looked into the living room. And I saw the guru.

He was sitting on the couch, sipping at a cup of coffee and joking around with Claudia. She laughed along as if they had forgotten why we were all assembled here. The blue camera bag sat in his lap, his free hand was sitting on top of it.

I stood there and watched him. He flirted to his left in German with Claudia and to his right in English with Evgenija, as if his whole life he had never done anything else. He was calling her Jenny already. I felt like grabbing him by the collar and throwing him out—he hadn't suffered any loss there.

He spotted me and the smile froze on his face. Had enough already, have you, I thought viciously. The next thought that occurred to me was a desire to accidentally trip on the strap of the camera bag and make it fall to the ground. We had good insurance. But he was sitting too far away and there was a rug at his feet.

He got up, put the camera in Mama Jenny's hands, and came over to me. He put out his hand. I thought for a second then shook it so as not to look like the most neurotic person around. He put his other hand on my shoulder. That really wasn't necessary.

"My condolences." He pulled me close and put an arm around me while his right hand continued to hold mine stuck between our stomachs.

"You already offered your condolences." I spoke in a formal tone. "Before I left, remember?"

"It doesn't matter." He finally let go of me. "Some things bear repeating."

"What are you doing here?"

"We decided to pay our respects to you and your family."

"Why didn't you call beforehand?"

"We kept calling your cell but nobody answered."

"That can't be true."

"That's what we thought. Which is why at some point I called your mother"—he took a bow in Claudia's direction—"only to find out that we had the number wrong on our telephone list the whole time. Then we decided to make a surprise visit."

"Who exactly is *we*?" My throat was raw, and my heart was pounding in my chest.

"All of us." He nodded to the side and smiled at me. "We all came to be here for you at the funeral."

"Who is *all of us*?" I wasn't stupid, I just couldn't believe it. I knew of no "we" that had anything to do with me. We had briefly created a little world together, us six cripples and the guru, but that time was over—I'd dropped out and was living in a completely different world now, one that revolved around death. I couldn't see where the two worlds could meet or why they even should. I felt as if someone I'd met on vacation had suddenly turned up at my home and asked me in front of everyone to rub sunscreen on her back.

"I didn't invite you." I stared at the camera.

"It's a funeral, you don't need an invitation," said a voice from behind me.

I turned around abruptly. Marlon was standing in the door to the patio.

"Were you sniffing the magnolias out there?" I asked full of hatred.

"The roses," he said with a polite smile. "The magnolias have already withered."

"And where are the rest of them? In the garage? In the closet?"

The guru was set on not losing his calm. "Why the closet?

They're at the hotel," he said evenly, smiling. "It means a lot to us to be able to support you."

Tammy hurried down the stairs, slipped, nearly fell, caught herself, straightened her back, and threw her head back. Her gaze fell with interest on Marlon.

"Why a hotel? We have enough rooms," she said.

I learned something important about myself in that moment. You could bite off my face and make me kiss my dead father but you had to leave me in peace otherwise, like in an attic room that nobody had access to except me. All that was over now, and I couldn't decide if I'd rather jump off the roof or smash all the dishes in the house.

Evgenija and Tammy, Janne and Kevin had sat down at the kitchen table and were cutting vegetables. I had lipstick on my cheek after Kevin's hello kiss; Richard took pity on me and told me. I tried to wipe it off but without a mirror it was tough, I probably just smeared it, in any event everyone just laughed themselves silly at me.

Janne had kissed me too. I bent down to her, she put her arm around my neck and brushed my cheek with her lips while I took a deep breath. It wasn't clear to me why I had missed her so little. I immediately forgave her for the fact that, compared to Claudia, she was pretty damn humorless. Anyone with eyes like hers didn't owe the world a thing. I looked at her with a mix of admiration and deep sympathy. The latter had to do with the conversation I'd had with Claudia in my room.

"Do you really think they came to support me?" I said. "You're all so naïve. The guru has other plans. Have you noticed his camera? He's making a movie. And a funeral like this makes a perfect scene."

"A movie?" asked Claudia curiously.

"I guess it's some sort of documentary," I explained. I didn't see any reason why I should cover for anyone. "He films at every opportunity. In the end some big secret will be revealed. Haven't you wondered why Janne is so nice to me? She thinks we make a perfect couple. She wants to be on the big screen, get it. She bounces back and forth between me and Marlon. Though I'm not sure if she's still doing that, maybe it was just part of the plan."

"Documentary film? Perfect couple?" Claudia sat down on my bed. Two lines formed across her forehead. I remembered that I used to put my fingers on those lines when I was a kid. "For what TV station?"

"No idea."

"Who's financing it?"

"No idea."

"Is there a treatment?"

"I haven't seen one."

"Did he tell you that he wanted to release it?"

"Um . . . no." I searched inside myself, trying to remember the things the guru had said to us. He himself had never actually said anything about a film. Friedrich had gushed about it right at the start, and I never doubted it because it sounded logical to me.

"I don't know what you all imagined," said Claudia. "He's making a few recordings, but they are definitely for private use, at the most for you guys to remember everything. But at your age everybody just wants to be famous. But now can you please explain to me again who is supposed to make a perfect couple?"

I felt as if somebody had just poured a bucket of ice-cold water over my head.

"Just forget it, please," I said. "It's just another misunderstanding."

The biggest misunderstanding of all, however, was the fact that they were all here. It was a nightmare. I resented Tammy's hospitality—at the end of the day I knew better than anyone that she was no nice little girl. And I couldn't understand why she suddenly had to act like one. Maybe she felt obligated to play the role of the widow.

As for Evgenija, I resented her because it suddenly turned out that she could speak German. Much better than I could speak English, not to mentioned Russian or Ukrainian.

"Laughable-but-passable," is how she described her ability. I stared at her like a talking donkey. "I had a German lover," she explained.

"I get it, it's a family tradition," I said in a polite tone. If everything was going to go off the rails, the least I could be was polite. Everyone was having fun and I didn't want to be the one they talked about later, the guy who showed no style at his father's funeral. The other person biding her time was Claudia. But she was only concerned with the guru, shadowing his every move; twice I caught them talking and falling silent as soon as I appeared. At least I didn't see the camera in his hand anymore.

Claudia was nice to everyone else. Too nice, I thought. She directed everything, counted rooms, pillows, and bodies, had cots moved into the study, and created a right mess. Tammy ran around with stacks of bedding. It turned out the guru had fibbed, as well. They hadn't checked into the hotel, he had just said that so as not to put any pressure on us.

I said very politely and clinically that it would be absolutely impossible for me to share the double bed in the attic with Marlon, as if we were a gay couple. I said that without my own room I would turn into a mass murderer. They all laughed. Janne and Tammy laughed the loudest. What I said interested them to a limited extent. What I wanted, not at all.

"Now pull yourself together," hissed Claudia after she'd plucked me out of the crowd and shoved me up against a wall. "I don't want my son of all people to act like a diva."

I gasped.

"Who's the diva here? I'm a diva? Have you seen the others? Do you have any . . . ?"

She punched me in the stomach, it was probably meant as an affectionate gesture, and all the breath still left in my lungs from my little speech rushed out into her face with a whistle. She turned away like I had bad breath.

"You can't mourn in peace around here anymore," I said. "There's a cripple in every corner."

"You're the only one here who's crippled." She pointed her finger at me like a pistol. "In your head."

"I've never denied that."

Claudia looked around as if she was afraid she'd be overheard.

"What I don't understand," I said with poorly disguised rage, "is why you all think it's so great. Especially you. At home you like to have your peace and quiet, too."

"I do not like to have my peace and quiet!" she shouted.

"Why isn't there ever anyone at our place then?"

"Because you and your carrying on have scared everyone off!" She no longer seemed to care whether anyone could hear her. "As long as we're living under one roof, I can't invite people over without you treating them in a way that I have to be ashamed of. None of them ever did anything to you, and you don't have to walk around like *weltschmerz* personified just because of a few scratches on your cheek. Yes, I like the fact that there are people here who want to be there for you even though you are the way you are. Let me finish," she said as I opened my mouth to object. "I know every word you're going to say before you say it. Naturally you want nothing to do with them. Naturally you're the only one out of all of them who isn't deranged. Naturally . . . " She ground to a halt mid-sentence and threw me a pitying look, as if I was no match for the clever words of her monologue. "And now shut your mouth and offer the guests something to drink."

We walked to the cemetery. It was nine in the morning and the church bells were ringing. The morning was autumnally cold and our feet waded through fog. Ferdi walked between Tammy and Evgenija. He kept lifting his legs and hanging from their hands. I watched them from behind, how heavy he was, how the arms of the two women tensed and their backs stiffened in order to keep him in the air. But they didn't say anything to him or to each other. Everyone looked straight ahead.

I'd been startled when I looked into Tammy's face early that morning. I was one of the first awake because it drove me crazy lying in bed next to a panting man. Claudia, who'd made coffee in industrial volume, sent me back upstairs to wake Tammy. I hadn't even knocked on Tammy's door before she suddenly opened it. I looked at the woman standing in the room, in a black dress and black tights, on skyscraper heels, who seemed to show no age at all but did have a certain facial expression. I wanted to have one just like it: serious and solemn and all-knowing. I felt like a kitchen knave who had just disturbed the queen. The wires crossed in my head and I choked back a "congratulations" before it very nearly escaped my lips. Then, just to be sure, I put my hand over my mouth.

She arched her eyebrows royally. A tiny hint of a smile hid on the right side of her mouth and I would really have liked to kiss it.

"Breakfast," I said hoarsely. "May I?" I offered an elbow and we went down the stairs side by side, and suddenly I thought: My father is a lucky son of a bitch. Living or dead—what difference did that make.

I looked at Tammy's straight back and the steady steps she took with her never-ending legs. I pushed Janne's wheelchair and knew she was looking at Tammy's legs, too. Her perspective allowed her to really scrutinize legs. Janne's black Snow White hair was up, held together by a hairclip made of dark horn with matte cut stones. I had no doubt that she hated Tammy. And I admired her for not showing it. The view of Janne's delicate, white, frail neck was unobstructed, and suddenly, for the first time in my life, I thought that people were more than their shells.

The thought was so striking that I turned to Friedrich, who was bringing up the rear. I'd already forgotten how his voice sounded. As soon as he arrived he'd gone up and built castles with Ferdi. I had hardly even noticed that he was there. I looked at him intently and realized that something about him had changed. I'd never experienced him silent. And he'd never worn a black leather jacket before. Had he gone shopping before the funeral? Or had he had that hidden in his suitcase the whole time?

He noticed that I was staring at him, and returned my gaze, serious and calm. I nodded to him—I hadn't really greeted him since his arrival—and kept walking.

"You see, good thing," said Claudia when we reached the cemetery walls.

"What's a good thing?"

"That we came on foot." She pointed at the cars lined up along the street. Countless limousines crawled down the street one after the next, and the long herky-jerky column went on and on without end. Our troop had already wound its way onto the pedestrian pathway to make way for the cars, only Janne and I were still blocking traffic.

"Excuse me," I said and shoved her onto the sidewalk as well.

She briefly rubbed her cheek against my hand on the grip.

The parking lot in front of the chapel had long since filled up and cars were parked two deep along the street. People were walking from every direction toward the entrance, in black dresses and long coats, and with their heads hanging. Some carried small bunches of flowers, others were lugging giant arrangements. I realized with a scalding hot flash that I didn't have a single flower with me. I wanted to ask Claudia why we were all assembled here—for a moment I actually forgot—and to remind her that we'd shown up empty-handed, all of us. But she had already reached the entrance to the chapel with Tammy and I could no longer make her out in the crowd of black dresses.

Obviously I'd been wrong. Obviously flowers had been prepared. On our chairs in the front row were little arrangements, three white roses bound together with a black ribbon, all the way across the entire row. In order to sit down you had to first pick up the flowers. One of my roses still had a thorn and I immediately cut myself on it. I stuck my finger in my mouth and licked the drops of blood as I heard Lucy's warnings echo in my ear about how all roses these days were treated with highly toxic pesticides. Lucy was interested in that sort of thing, genetically modified food and animal testing and poor farmers in South America. I had always pretended that I too was interested in that stuff. In reality I'd only been interested in myself, even back then. My vision started to blur so I shut my eyes and concentrated on the salty taste in my mouth.

The party was in full swing. Not quite as many people had come as had been expected, it had been the invitation to the home, *people inclined to maintain a comfortable distance were put off by the intimacy*, that's what Evgenija yelled disappointedly in my ear in the kitchen. But actually it was good because nearly everyone had a place to sit.

"Awesome!!!" I shouted back in her ear. I'd thrown my arm around her neck and pulled her tightly to me because there was an incredible din that was either in the house or maybe just in my head. The little pearl earrings in her earlobes brushed the tip of my nose; I nearly bit them but I just missed them. Evgenija laughed and removed my arm. I choked on the cloud of perfume she left behind. I didn't know exactly how many of the tiny glasses I'd downed, two or five, I'd done it just like Tammy had taught me: don't think, don't clink glasses, down the hatch, and a little something afterwards. My throat was burning. I hadn't felt so light for a long time.

Evgenija had tied a red apron over her black outfit. Claudia's striped skirt was barely a centimeter longer. It took effort to distinguish them from each other through the haze of cigarette smoke. They stood at the stove, stirred the pots, pulled baking sheets out of the oven, and ordered Tammy around. Tammy didn't listen to them. She moved through the babble of conversation like a fish in an aquarium, a smile on her face that made me worry. She kept stopping and sitting down next to one of the handpicked guests. Maybe she was confusing a funeral for a champagne reception.

Some of the men she talked with seemed familiar, one I recognized as the mayor who had held the office since I was a child, another I'd seen in a TV interview, he'd defended a twisted murderer. They kissed Tammy's hands, put their knotty old man hands on the back of her head, held her girlish forehead against their black-clad shoulders, paused for a while, let her go again, and looked with mournful eyes down at her cleavage. A few of them blew their noses loudly into bath-towel-size monogrammed handkerchiefs. Why were they all bawling, I wondered. Until I remembered again.

It was difficult to move through the room. There were tables and chairs and benches all over the place, same thing outside in the garden, but I couldn't stay in one place, I just followed Tammy around. I was afraid that something awful might happen, and wanted to try to head anything off before it went too far. I tripped over handbags and outstretched legs, once I fell into Kevin's lap and he hugged me and wiped my cheeks with the back of his hand.

"What an amazing foster dad you had!" he said, and his smeared eyelashes hung heavy with mascara teardrops.

"Excuse me?" I made a halfhearted effort to straighten myself back up, but my legs didn't want to hold me. "What are you talking about?"

"He must have been unbelievable."

"You're drunk. You didn't even know him."

"If he wasn't so amazing then all these people wouldn't have come."

"He was a lawyer, Kevin. These are clients and colleagues. They know how to be respectful."

"No." He shook his head and strange particles of ash scattered onto my black jacket from his hair.

I finally managed to stand up, leaving my hand on his shoulder.

"I'm really touched that you all came," I slurred. "Really."

"I know," Kevin answered with glazed eyes. "We'd never leave you in the lurch."

That scared me so much that I excused myself and moved on, following Tammy. I had to pass Janne and practically climbed over her wheelchair—she was deep in conversation with the mayor, who looked up at me and with a furrowed brow squinted at my face as if he was asking himself whether he was dreaming.

"Don't let me interrupt," I said, leaning down to Janne and planting a kiss on her lips. The expected slap didn't materialize, she was probably too surprised. I let Janne go and righted myself again so I could focus on her face better.

"She's the most beautiful girl I've ever seen," I explained to the mayor.

He smiled politely. Janne took my hand and squeezed it. I was a half-orphan now and she was a good friend, there was nothing illicit in the gesture and the mayor looked on benevolently.

"Do you think a girl like this could love a monster like me?" I asked a touch too loudly.

He smiled even more politely. Janne let go of my hand and pushed me away with both arms, though it didn't come across as angry, more like playfully intimate. I kissed her head, found my balance with effort, and headed off.

I found Richard and Friedrich in the garden. Claudia had lit the torches and put a huge ashtray out. I joined them, took a cigarette out of Richard's chest pocket, and peered into Friedrich's face.

"How are you?" he asked. It wasn't so much that I heard it as I read it on his lips.

"Very well. I have to ask you guys something." I put my arm around Friedrich's shoulders and pulled him near. This was no longer one of my moves; before, more than a year ago, I used to do it regularly, with boys and girls, and they always liked it when I grabbed them, my touch was quick and coveted. Friedrich didn't want to be pulled closer now. He stood steadily on his legs and his lips pursed. Then he twisted his arms so he could give me a friendly pat on the shoulder and free himself from my embrace.

"What did you guys do with him?" I asked Richard and pointed to Friedrich. "You can't even recognize him. He was a fat chatterbox and now, just a few days later . . . Friedrich, has your hair gotten gray?"

He smiled. "It's just the light. The guru revealed something to us," he said.

"Do tell."

He hesitated.

"Is it about you?"

"About you, too."

"Oh." For a moment I was almost sober again. Suddenly I wanted to call Claudia and ask her to put me to bed. Instead I said as calmly as possible, "So? Can you summarize it for me?"

"We're not the people we always thought we were."

I looked back and forth between him and Richard. They continued to look at me impassively.

"And that's why you are different now than before," I managed to grind out.

"I always was," said Friedrich. "I just didn't know it."

"And what's the story with me? Can you tell me?"

And then he told me.

I reached behind me for a wall to brace my suddenly wobbly spine against. Unfortunately I didn't find one.

"Thanks for the talk," I said and staggered away.

I puttered around the garden for a long time. It got cooler and the guests retreated to the house, jamming the place up to the last hallway until there was no place else left to stand. I could see them through the fogged up window. The black clothes melted into a single mass, the faces slowly lost their mournfulness. Here and there I could make out familiar facial features. At one stage I jumped because I thought I saw Lucy. The sound of the voices condensed into a single ill-defined cloud that sent out occasional thunderclaps of laughter. Suddenly I heard guitar chords accompanied by other tones that I couldn't immediately place. I pressed my nose to the glass and saw an accordion.

Evgenija was sitting on the table; the musical instrument that I had at first taken for some kind of animal whined ruefully in her lap. Her left foot hung in the air; the high-heeled shoe had slipped down. A massive knee in black pants, whose owner I couldn't make out, pushed under Evgenija's toes to brace them as they felt around in the air.

She couldn't start singing along now too, I thought, but right at that moment she showed that indeed she could. I couldn't see who was playing guitar. I just hoped it wasn't Claudia.

I stepped back from the window. If someone inside saw me like that, his or her hair would immediately turn white. I needed to show some regard for the guests. A maniacal grin wafted across my face. I went farther into the garden, cut my shoe on a piece of broken glass in the grass, and then I saw that someone was standing next to me.

"Tammy," I said. "You're dressed too lightly again."

At the funeral she'd worn a jacket over her short black dress even though it was fairly warm. Now she no longer had the jacket on, and didn't have shoes on her feet. Maybe it was a Ukrainian custom to go barefoot at some stage during a funeral.

She took a step toward me and I searched for her face, first with my fingers and then with my lips. Her skin tasted bitter then sweet then both at the same time. I pulled away from her because my stomach started to growl.

"Can't you wash that off?"

"You're drunk," she said.

"Never," I said. I pulled a crumpled tissue out of my pocket, spat on it, and tried to wipe Tammy's mouth with it. She pushed my hand aside.

I held her so she didn't run away from me and get lost in her own garden. She nuzzled up to me. Maybe she was just cold.

"It's a killer funeral," I said. "You guys really did a great job putting it together. The food, incredible."

"Did you try it?"

"No," I said. "But I really need to tell you that you picked super music for the ceremony. I nearly cried."

"That was Claudia's music," said Tammy into my shirt. "I can burn you a CD."

"No, thanks," I said quickly. "I don't listen to music."

I stroked her hair. My finger got caught in a curl, my fingertips were raw and cracked like those of a laborer. I stroked her head with the flat of my hand, the way you pat a child or a dog. Then I kissed her head and her temples, which smelled like smoke and her unbearable perfume. She wrapped both arms around me and we stood there like that, as if nothing on earth could part us.

"Tammy," I said. "I have to confess something to you."

She lifted her face inquisitively.

"You see that girl in there?"

"The snow queen in the wheelchair?"

"Exactly."

"What about her?"

"I love her," I said.

Tammy nodded. I'd been a little worried that it would hurt her feelings that I was kissing her here in the garden and confessing my love of another woman at the same time. If I'd been just a touch more sober I would have kept my mouth shut.

"You all have a crush on that girl." Tammy sounded totally indifferent. "The guests are all smitten. I thought they'd all try to start something with me, but as soon as she showed up . . . I wonder how she does it. I don't think she's really paralyzed."

"No idea," I said. "It actually doesn't even matter."

I stroked her head again as she leaned against my shoulder.

"*I'd* like to start something with you," I said.

"Why? You have a chance with that girl."

"Nice of you, but not a chance in hell, Tammy. I think I'm going crazy. People are trying to tell me weird things. Look for example at that girl in the wheelchair again. Do we look similar?"

"Maybe."

"But she has black hair."

"It's dyed, you idiot."

"No," I said. Even though I immediately believed her.

She reached out her hand and tussled my hair. "I think you and your friends all look a little alike."

"You did not just say that!"

"You're so sweet, and the princess must have understood immediately that you two would make a very effective couple."

"What are you talking about?"

She suddenly shrunk back and pushed me toward the house. "Go talk to her," she said.

The feeling of loss I felt when she slid out of my arms was insufferable. And I wasn't planning to suffer it. I pulled her back to me.

"I love her but I'm afraid of her," I said. "She's a much worse monster than I am. And even though I know that, it still pulls at me when I look at her. I want to take her in my arms and carry her through the world so she doesn't have to cry anymore. So nobody has to cry anymore."

"You're a true superhero," said Tammy, and as hard I tried I couldn't hear any sarcasm in her voice this time.

I have no idea how much longer we stood there in the garden before I hit on the idea to put my hand under her dress and realized when I did that her ass was ice-cold.

"Let's go inside," I said and we walked around the house. We didn't want to go in by the patio because there were too many people standing there, and the front door was also no good, it was completely blocked. Tammy took me around another corner, on the side of the house, to a spiral staircase. The steps wobbled and creaked feebly beneath our feet, but then we were standing in my attic room, though my joy was premature. Marlon was lying in the double bed. Next to him was Ferdi.

"Ferdi!" screamed Tammy shrilly. I'd bet anything that she'd completely forgotten him. She'd forgotten that she even had a son. Ferdi didn't wake up, but Marlon could no longer pretend he was asleep.

"He wanted to come with me," he said. And the helplessness in his voice was as ill-suited to him as the look on his face, the same look he'd had on his face at the train station when we left Berlin for Marenitz. "Then he fell asleep here."

Tammy rocked back and forth and stared at Marlon with her eyes wide open. He smiled pitifully past her.

"It's fine," I said and lifted Ferdi up. He was sweaty again and smelled like rye bread. I nuzzled his hair then nodded at

Marlon as if he could see, wished him goodnight, and carried Ferdi down to his room.

"I want to have one of my own someday," I said after Tammy had tucked in her son and pulled the door to his room closed from outside.

"Take this one," said Tammy.

I wasn't planning to sleep at all. How would it even be possible with the noise downstairs coming through the floor of Tammy's bedroom, it was so loud that I was afraid it might lift up the floor. I didn't think anyone could hear anything. I was woozy, the walls were spinning, we were all over one another, everywhere all at the same time, I couldn't tell up from down. It felt like gravity had dissipated and I was stuck to the ceiling like a fly, and I kept reaching my hand out to Tammy until she pulled away and squeezed a pillow between us.

"That's enough," she said brusquely. "I can't take anymore."

I found it sweet that she thought a pillow could stop me. I pulled it away and threw it toward where I assumed the floor was. I pressed her forehead to my shoulder the way the guys with graying temples dressed in black had done downstairs in the living room. She was wet and salty from head to toe. I wondered why she was still trembling. Then I realized she was crying, and I couldn't do anything but hold her in my arms and wait until it stopped. I did it with every ounce of patience I had in me, and didn't think once about how much would finally be enough.

I woke up when Claudia knocked on the door and asked if Tammy knew where I was. Tammy lay with her face in the pillow, all I could see were bushels and bushels of tangled hair. I gently shook her shoulder, nothing happened. For a second I thought about how Claudia would react if I answered.

I waited until Claudia's footsteps retreated, then kissed Tammy on her left shoulder blade, right where a lizard was tattooed. She mumbled something and tried to hit me and caught my nose with her elbow. Then she sat abruptly up in bed. With her smeared face she looked a bit like a clown.

She looked at me and her eyes cleared. Then she jumped out of bed.

"You have to get out of here!"

I sighed. She peered into the hallway and then shoved me out of the room.

I ran up to the attic. The clothes that I'd grabbed off the floor and thrown on stuck to my skin. The fact that Marlon would be waiting for me under the roof didn't bother me. I wanted to tell him everything. Since he couldn't even see me, it would make it easier. Then he'd say something and I could go on with my life.

Marlon wasn't there. His travel bag wasn't there. The bed was made. On the nightstand was one of my socks.

I stumbled down the stairs.

"Claudia! What the hell?"

The kitchen was empty.

I ran through the rooms. Where the tables had stood, the tiles were gleaming again. The dishwasher was on. I scratched the back of my neck. Then I went upstairs again and looked in all the rooms except Tammy's. Nobody was there. No Friedrich, no Richard. No sign of Janne. Not even Claudia or Evgenija. And no Ferdi.

This must have been what it felt like to go crazy.

I heard a scraping noise out in the garden. I opened the patio door and immediately wished I could close it again. But he had already turned around.

"Hello, Dirk," I said, jammed in the half-open door.

He was holding a huge blue plastic bag in his hands. He leaned down and picked something up and tossed it into the bag. I had the feeling that I'd already been part of a similar scene a few days before.

"I didn't know that you were here." I shielded my face from the sun with my hand. Only now did I realize I'd forgotten my sunglasses. I apologized.

"No problem." He looked at me in a way meant to telegraph how cool he was with it. "We actually spoke yesterday."

"Really?" Out of surprise I took my hand away from my face.

"Of course. I'm sorry I wasn't able to come earlier to help out. I had to be in court, there was no way around it."

"No problem," I said repeating his words. "And you were here the whole time yesterday?"

He let the bag drop to the ground and came up the steps onto the patio. He put out his arms and hugged me so tightly I had to fight for air.

"Let me say this again in peace and quiet. I'm very sorry. Your father must have been a wonderful man. I feel for you guys."

I nodded, then freed myself and gratefully created a bit of space between us. He went back to the garbage bag.

"Wait!" I called, worried that he too might disappear into thin air. I wanted to ask him about the others but I didn't know how.

At that moment I heard the familiar sound of tires on the gravel driveway, car doors closing, the click of heels on the flagstones.

"Breakfast!" called Evgenija and Claudia simultaneously.

Ferdi had asked whether we could eat on the patio. I hadn't heard him ask for anything during all the time I'd been here. Together with Dirk I carried a round table out. Claudia filled a bamboo bowl with rolls and croissants from a paper bag as big as a child.

"Uh," I said. "Where are my . . . " She looked at me. I didn't know how to ask her about them. If she realized how hysterical I was becoming she'd definitely start worrying.

"Your . . . ?"

"Yes."

She smiled with her broad mouth. Her eyetooth was red with lipstick. "They had to catch an early train. We took them to the station in two cars. Where did you sleep? The only room we didn't look for you in was the garage. Is that where you were?"

"Yeah."

She jabbed me in the ribs. I held her hand.

"Claudia," I said. "I don't deserve you."

"I know." She put marmalade jars on a tray and handed it to me. The milk and coffee pot she gave to Dirk, who was waiting next to me.

"Now go," she said to him because he didn't budge and was standing there staring at her with his mouth open. "Have you never seen me before or what?"

I went out quickly. Ferdi was tipping back on his chair the same way I always used to. But he couldn't yet do it very well.

He looked as if he might tip over at any second and hit his head on the stone slabs. I tried to imagine what would happen then. I grabbed his chair at the exact point that it started to go over. Ferdi didn't even realize he was going to fall. He was annoyed until I picked him up and put him on my shoulders.

"Stay," said Ferdi from above. "All the others need to go, but you should stay."

"I'll stay," I said. "Another whole day."

In the end I stayed two days, a whole day longer than Claudia and Dirk, a half day longer than Tammy's mother. Claudia and Dirk had to work. Dirk waited next to the open passenger door while Claudia hugged first Tammy and then her mother. Then she put her arms out toward me, reconsidered, and pinched my cheek.

"You don't always have to hurt me, Mother," I said.

She peered into my eyes and shook her head as if I'd done something wrong again. As if I'd done everything in my life wrong. Everyone watched closely. This wasn't the moment to ask her questions.

"Drive carefully," I said and then they were gone.

Mama Jenny kept practicing a Russian poem with Ferdi right up to her departure. I didn't ask whether I should go with her to the airport. Ferdi didn't go, either. I held him in my arms as if he was three instead of six so his Ukrainian grandmother could kiss him goodbye without bending down. I couldn't shake the feeling that she still looked at him skeptically, like there was something that bothered her about him. In essence she looked at him the same way Claudia looked at me.

She kissed me three times on the cheek then, with an impish smile, she ripped off my sunglasses.

It took my breath away.

She tossed the glasses to her feet and stepped on first one lens and then the other with her heels. The glass shattered. Evgenija swept the shards aside with her foot and got into the car as Tammy honked impatiently. Tammy didn't see a thing. I put Ferdi down. He avoided looking at me.

"That grandma, huh?" I said. I was happy to be alone for a moment at last. Nearly alone. Ferdi leaned against my legs and oddly enough it didn't bother me one bit.

We were both asleep on the couch when Tammy got home. I sensed her shadow on my face even through my new glasses, and woke up.

"Your mother isn't too thrilled about your career as a gold digger, eh?" I whispered because Ferdi was still asleep. "She no doubt had great hopes for you, a distinguished academic track, and now you're just sitting around in this crap town going gaga. Tell me I'm wrong."

"It's none of your business. Is this yours?"

"Did you try to trick him? Did you want to stay in Germany? But the era when a girl like you would be willing to get pregnant so easily is long gone. When I saw your mother I knew immediately that you didn't need to do that."

"*He* tricked *me*," said Tammy wearily. "He was apparently sure he was sterile. I thought maybe he'd had a vasectomy after you. A child was the last thing I wanted. And now he's gone forever and I'm left to dole out the soup. So tell me, is this yours?"

Now I noticed that Tammy was holding a medium-sized blue bag in her hands.

"No."

"Did Claudia forget it maybe?"

"Maybe." Then I sat up and carefully pushed Ferdi's feet off my groin and took the bag. I knew immediately who it belonged to. My heart was in my mouth.

"I'll call her," I mumbled, pushing past Tammy and running upstairs.

I locked the door and put a chair in front of it. I sat down on the bed, but it didn't seem secure enough so I sat on the chair blocking the door. I closed my eyes, felt around for the zipper, and opened the bag. Then I pulled out the camera, turned it on, and pushed play.

Hello, people," said the guru into the lens, smiling feebly. The camera seemed to wobble in his hands, the picture was awful, and his facial expression was strained. He pulled his hat frantically off his head. The camera shook even worse. Instead of turning it off I stared with wide eyes at the display.

"Hello, children," said the guru and something happened to his eyes. They glazed over strangely. I felt a sense of embarrassment well up in me. I didn't think men should cry.

"Hello, dear children," said the guru. "You know by now that you aren't my only ones. You're just my . . . the most interesting. I love you all. You don't have to believe me. You have no reason to trust me. But I can sleep a little easier knowing that you at least have each other."

The camera slipped out of my hands and I grabbed it back. There wasn't much to see. The guru looked at me from the display and cried. I shifted impatiently in my seat.

"Don't think too poorly of me," he finally managed to say.

At that moment my thumb pushed the fast-forward button. I didn't want to hear him anymore.

The guru's face grimaced in fast-motion. It was impossible to tell whether he was talking or just silently stewing over his thoughts. His hand flew up to his forehead, the hat landed back on his head at some point and then was taken off again.

I had no patience. I slowed the playback to normal speed again when Janne's face appeared. Janne in the garden next to

Marlon, who was running his finger along the wheel of her wheelchair, a gesture that made me turn red. One of the first recordings we did together. They looked good, both of them. But it didn't help them. If the guru had his way they would be each other's half-siblings.

And mine as well.

I leaned my head back and laughed myself sick.

They were nice recordings, blurry but atmospheric, they looked as if they'd been shot decades ago rather than last week. The kind of movies you showed your grandchildren. That's me as a child. Right there I'm traveling with my . . . uh . . . never mind. That's your great-aunt Janne. She was so pretty then. And Marlon would have surely broken my nose that day if he wasn't as blind as a mole. I got lucky. What happened to your great-uncle Friedrich, you'll have to ask him yourselves, I never understood it. Here he still looks like a cheap teddy bear won at the funfair. For some reason he'd planned to off himself back then but then he'd reconsidered. Maybe he'd found out he couldn't have had the inherited diseases he'd embraced up to then.

My finger swept along the camera bag. It had a few side pockets, something was crackling inside, I pulled it out because I thought at first it felt like money. But it was just a piece of paper, folded up several times to make it very small. I unfolded it and smoothed it out.

It was a list of names. Quite a lot of names, with numbers next to them, and next to those, in parentheses, women's names. Birth dates: they started three years before mine and ended two years later. Mothers and their children. It was easy to find our six. They were all marked with stars.

I didn't want anyone to think I had friends. Certainly not friends like them. We would never be friends. In reality it was far worse. In reality everything was far worse. And weirder.

I couldn't find a doorbell so I knocked with my fist and pushed it open. I still remembered how I always walked by this place on the way to kindergarten. The smell of horses and straw crept under the door and out onto the street and had intoxicated me. Sometimes I'd stopped and waited for the door to finally open and a horse that I was sure lived there to come out. But it never happened, not a single time.

"Come in!" called a woman's voice but I was already inside.

She was small and round and had a smile that reminded me of Lucy. She was about fifty, maybe older. She looked at me a little surprised; I held up my fist which was clutching the flyer I'd taken off the wall in front of the grocery store.

"Are they still here?"

"Of course. All of them." She smiled again and led me to the stall. There stood a workbench, and next to it were stacks of wood. A huge wagon wheel entwined with ivy hung on the wall.

"Here." The woman grabbed me carefully by the sleeve when I started in the wrong direction. She put a few crumbling foul-smelling lumps in my hand. "Give it to the mother."

The mother licked my hand after I held out the lumps. Her tickly warm tongue sought out any remaining crumbs between my fingers. She had a pointy nose and bright eyes. Three fat babies ran toward me howling and bustled about my feet.

"All three?" The woman looked at me for a moment and then turned her face to the sun again. I squatted down to pet the mother.

"No," I said. "Only two, unfortunately."

She handed me a beat-up wicker basket, lined it with a tattered wool blanket, and together we trapped two of the puppies, a reddish one and another with black spots, and set them in the basket. They nudged each other and whimpered. The woman said something about chips and vaccinations but I didn't listen. I petted the puppies. Then I handed the woman a hundred euros.

She took the money and put it in the pocket on the front of her apron.

"I can't just give them away. Things that don't cost anything don't have any value." She sounded as if she was trying to apologize.

"I know," I said. "You're totally right."

The mother wagged her tail as if she couldn't think of anything nicer than being freed of two of her children. I petted her one last time. The woman took me to the door.

"I'm sorry about your father," she said when I was back out on the street. "Peace to his soul."

"Thanks," I said.

"I would have recognized you anyway, though," she said. "You used to come past here all the time on the way to kindergarten."

She seemed to be waiting for an answer, but I stood there mute with the basket of puppies pressed to my chest. Then she smiled one last time and closed the door, and I hadn't asked her if she'd ever really had a horse in the stalls.

A re you crazy?" shouted Tammy. "How do you see it working?"

"I promised him," I said.

"You're a regular superhero—you promise things and then I'm the bad guy. How dare you? What am I supposed to feed it?"

"I'll pay for the food," I said. "And I'll take him whenever you go on vacation."

"That's easy to say!"

We both turned at the same time to the window. Ferdi was running through the garden. The puppies waddled after him and yelped excitedly. When I saw Ferdi's face I had to look away to avoid having something burst inside me. I threw a glance at Tammy. Tears were running down her face, but she was smiling.

"Come with me to Berlin," I said. "You don't have to stay here. I'll take care of you. As best I can."

She shook her head.

"What's keeping you here?"

"You wouldn't understand. And who is the second one for?" she asked huffily. "For you?"

I shrugged. For some reason I didn't want to tell her. Maybe she'd get jealous. Maybe that was just a bunch of nonsense.

"It's going be an awesome trip," said Tammy impishly on the train platform. "I hope the doggy pisses all over you and you get into trouble with the other passengers."

"No doubt about it," I consoled her.

She didn't ask if I could stay any longer. It raised her in my esteem. I hugged her and inhaled deeply and then heard her whisper hoarsely in my ear.

"I'll always love him."

"I know."

I jostled with the door to the regional train that had rattled into the station. A mere six hours and two transfers later I'd be home. I found an empty compartment and put the basket with the puppy down on the seat. Above the headrest was a scratched mirror. The basket began to rock precariously so I put it down on the ground. Then I opened the window and leaned out.

"Go home," I said to Tammy, who was standing on the platform in her short dress shivering.

She nodded and didn't budge. It would have been better if she had left. As it was I couldn't really sit down, I had to look at her and wonder whether she was waiting out of a sense of obligation and was actually thinking about how much each extra minute of parking was costing her. But she persevered until the train pulled away and then waved and I waved back. Then I couldn't see her anymore.

The puppy had managed to climb out of the basket. He discovered my shoe and wagged his little tail so eagerly you'd think he had been missing that shoe his entire life. I caught him again and put him back in the basket.

Air was being sucked out the window. I closed it and threw my suitcase up on the luggage rack. I was looking forward to Claudia. I had a few things to say to her. But I had a feeling that by the time I got to Berlin my big speech would have dwindled to just a few words.

And I wouldn't say them anyway.

I turned toward the mirror and took off my glasses.